Hoofb...

Katie and the Mustang

Book Two

by KATHLEEN DUEY

PUFFIN BOOKS

PUFFIN BOOKS
Published by Penguin Group
Penguin Young Readers Group, 345 Hudson Street,
New York, New York 10014, U.S.A.
Penguin Books Ltd, 80 Strand, London WC2R ORL, England
Penguin Books Australia Ltd, 250 Camberwell Road,
Camberwell, Victoria 3124, Australia
Penguin Books Canada Ltd, 10 Alcorn Avenue,
Toronto, Ontario, Canada M4V 3B2
Penguin Books (N.Z.) Ltd, 182-190 Wairau Road,
Auckland 10, New Zealand

Published simultaneously in the United States of America by Dutton Children's
Books and Puffin Books, divisions of Penguin Young Readers Group, 2004

1 3 5 7 9 10 8 6 4 2

Puffin Books ISBN 0-14-240091-2

Printed in the United States of America

My childhood memories are set to hoofbeats:
a fog-softened gallop on a lonely morning; the joyous
clatter of friends pounding down the Canal Road;
a measured, hollow clop of a miles-to-go July afternoon;
the snow-muffled hoofbeats of wintertime; the squelching
rhythm of a close race with a rainstorm. These books
are for my dear friends, the horses of my childhood—
Buck, Ginger, Steve, and Cherokee Star.

Thank you all.

CHAPTER ONE

❦ ❦ ❦

*It was pure joy to be beneath the sky once more,
to have the other horses for company, to stand with them
every night under the stars. The little one led
the way and stayed close. Her voice and hands were always
soft, always gentle.*

*T*he night was nearly silent, just the sound of frogs and crickets, until it got really chilly; then they hushed, and all that was left was the creaking of Hiram's wagon and the clopping of the horses' hooves.

That first night, all I wanted was to get as far from Mr. Stevens as I could. But after we passed the home place, I kept wondering what my parents would have told me, if they had lived. Would they think I was foolish to leave Scott County? It was surely safer to stay somewhere in the valley. But where? With who?

I held tight to the Mustang's lead rope as we walked down the dark road, my thoughts a hopeless snarl. I was scared. I was really afraid of setting out on my own like this, with only Hiram for company. But I couldn't see any other choice.

I couldn't go back. Not ever. Mr. Stevens had lied to me about everything. He had never meant to take me or the Mustang west. He'd planned on leaving me at a home for orphans in St. Louis, and he had told Hiram to shoot the Mustang. I kicked at the dirt. How could he just *lie* to me like that?

The Mustang tossed his head, startled when I kicked at the ground. I reached up to touch his cheek. "Mr. Stevens thought you were too wild to handle," I whispered. "He never even tried."

For a few seconds, I hated Mr. Stevens so much it made my teeth clench and turned my hands into fists. Even so, walking in the dark, I thought about going back, asking the McCarty family if I could stay with them after Mr. and Mrs. Stevens left. Then I shook my head.

They had little children, and they had seen the Mustang fighting to get out of the stall. They wouldn't want a dangerous half-wild horse on the place, even if they would have agreed to take in an orphan. And I didn't know them. They seemed nice. But the Stevenses had seemed nice at first, too.

I looked up at the scatter of stars overhead. "I'm scared," I told the Mustang. He twitched his ears and touched my shoulder with his muzzle as we went on, clopping along after the wagon.

An hour or two before dawn, Hiram reined the mares to the right and found a flat place to stop the wagon. He unhitched them and tethered them to the planked rails that enclosed the bed of the wagon. The Mustang seemed content to stand and doze beside Delia and Midnight. I tied him loosely, hoping he wouldn't get startled and fight the rope.

We made our pallets from canvas tarps and blankets Hiram had brought. Mine was in the wagon bed on top of some of our supplies. Hiram made his on the ground beneath the wagon.

Hiram slept; I could hear him snoring. The Mustang was quiet and still. But I lay awake in the bed of the farm wagon, worries still pinwheeling in my mind. What if the Oregon land wasn't as good as Mr. Barrett had said when he was talking people into going with him? After all, people paid him to take them west. What if he was lying to get their money? I wanted Hiram to find good land. He'd worked so hard for the Stevenses and had been so kind to me.

I wondered if my uncle Jack had hired a guide. Not that it mattered very much now. However he had gotten to Oregon, he'd had time to get a farm started, so at least once I found him, I wouldn't have to worry.

I kept watching the dark shape of the Mustang, afraid some night sound would startle him awake. I knew he might panic if he backed up or reared and felt the pull of the rope—but he didn't. He dozed quietly all night. I was the only one who couldn't sleep. It was a relief when the sky grayed with dawn and Hiram woke.

"I want to show you something," Hiram said once he'd started a little fire to boil his coffee. "I don't want to go east to Muscatine." He got a stick, then scuffed a patch of dirt bare so that he could draw a map.

I stood close to the fire and shivered while he talked. It was chilly, but the shivers came from deep inside me. Mr. Stevens had laid out the route: farm wagons to Muscatine, then a steamboat to St. Louis. The smaller, half-size Conestoga wagons that people called prairie schooners would be bought there, along with supplies. Then the trek across Missouri would end in Independence. Most people began the journey westward there—leaving as early as spring would allow. But Hiram was describing an altogether different route.

"This makes more sense for us," Hiram said, scratching lines in the dirt. "Straight west, hitting the old Fort Kearny Road, then on into Kanesville at Council Bluff to cross the Missouri." I stared at his stick-scratch map and tried to still my fears.

It did make sense. The whole reason for the Stevenses going south down the Mississippi River had been to carry their household goods. Hiram had less than half a wagon full—and I only had a blanket bundle.

I exhaled slowly, giving in to my worries. What if the wagon wasn't strong enough to make it all the way to Oregon? It was just a four-wheeled farm wagon, with iron-rimmed wheels as tall as I was that creaked and groaned over every bump in the road. The leather shoe on the wooden brake was worn, and the singletree chains were rusted. The original plan had been to leave this wagon in Muscatine and board a steamship south to St. Louis. That's where the special wagons were sold, the ones built to take the steep rocky trails Mr. Barrett had talked about.

"Is this wagon stout enough?" I asked quietly.

Hiram nodded. "I think so, for what we have in it. I had the axles replaced with white oak, and the wheels are sound." He looked at it, narrowing his eyes. "And we're not hauling much, even once we add provisions and such."

"So where do we start the journey, then?" I asked him.

Hiram turned to look at me. "Council Bluff. Lots of wagon companies form up there, too."

"Did Mr. Barrett talk about Council Bluff?" I asked Hiram.

He shook his head. "No. But his party was forming up in Independence."

I nodded slowly. "But a lot of people leave from Council Bluff?"

Hiram nodded patiently at my needing to hear it twice. "And the Mormon families are camped there now, people say, several thousand of them."

I wasn't sure what Mormon meant, but I was too tired to ask, and, to be honest, I didn't really care just then—it was how many that amazed me. I tried to imagine several thousand people all in one place. I couldn't.

Hiram tossed the coffee grounds out of his cup and stretched. "We'll sleep more tonight, I hope."

I nodded. I wasn't sure I had slept at all for worrying. My eyes felt sandy, and I longed for water to splash on my face. Feeling uneasy, I helped Hiram harness the team, then rolled the canvas tarps and put them in the wagon. The Mustang seemed calm enough, though I could tell that he didn't like being separated from the wagon team. He nuzzled my cheek, and I could feel his warm breath in my hair.

Hiram climbed onto the driver's bench, and I took my place behind the wagon.

"Ready, Katie?"

"I am," I answered, and the wagon wheels creaked into life as the mares leaned into the harness. I held the stallion back for a few paces, so we would have a little room for him to shy or skitter if he needed to, then I started forward. The Mustang followed me without hesitation, and I looked up at him.

His honey-colored coat was dark dun in the dim light before dawn. Hiram held the mares to a walk, and I kept up fairly easily.

By midmorning, I was less scared. There is something about sunlight that chases worries away, at least for a while. There is also something comforting about the heartbeat sound of hooves on a dirt road—or at least there was for me. Every mile we traveled was a mile closer to Uncle Jack and a real family, a real home.

I had been right to leave a few steps of spare room between us and the wagon. The Mustang pranced and danced that whole morning, his tail high and his neck arched. I had to run alongside him sometimes, but he was careful of me. He watched me—and so did Hiram.

"All right back there?" he kept asking over his shoulder.

"Fine!" I answered every time, even though I was scared that the Mustang's high spirits would send him galloping across the endless prairie grass. There were no farms in sight, nothing but open land from one horizon to the other. If he got away from me, it was possible I would never see him again. The thought made my heart ache.

I clutched at the lead rope so hard that for the first three days I had painful hand cramps. Blisters raised up on my skin from holding the rope so tight.

Every day we traveled, the Mustang would get skittish at times. His head would go up, and he would scent the wind, and I could see a wildness come into his eyes. He would half rear and kick his heels, and I would hang on desperately, talking to him in as calm a voice as I could manage. On the sixth day a coyote startled us, running across the road. The Mustang reared and jerked the rope, and the blisters on my hands broke. It stung like fire, but after a few sore days, my palms hardened into calluses.

"You all right back there?" Hiram called out when he heard the Mustang's hoofbeats clatter.

"I'm fine," I called back. I always told him that, even if it wasn't quite true. I didn't want him to decide that the Mustang was too much trouble, or get worried about me getting hurt.

"You sure you got a real good hold on that animal?" Hiram shouted back to me one warm afternoon. His voice broke hours of silence, and I was startled out of my thoughts.

"I do," I answered.

"Can you hold him tight, you think?"

"I can," I answered, my heart speeding up. "Why?"

He clucked at the team, then turned and spoke over his shoulder again. "We've got a pretty good creek to cross up ahead."

I reached up to lay my hand on the Mustang's neck. Some horses hated to cross water. "You must have crossed lots of creeks and rivers back on your home range," I whispered.

He lifted his head and flared his nostrils, and I wondered if he was just then scenting the water. I pressed the palm of my hand on his neck. If I couldn't get him across, what would Hiram do? What would *I* do?

"You going to wade, Katie? Or sit on the wagon gate?" Hiram asked.

I didn't answer because I wasn't sure. I couldn't see around the wagon, and I didn't want to lead the Mustang to the side so that I could. He might bolt if the wagon wasn't squarely in front of us.

I tried to think. Would the Mustang try to pull free if I were bouncing along on the back of the wagon? He wasn't what anyone would call halter-broke—not in any real way. He was following me because he liked me and because he was grateful to be out of the stall that had been his prison. He didn't imagine for one second that I was strong enough to hold him if he tried to bolt. Neither did I.

"He's used to me walking close," I told Hiram. "How high is the water?"

"Never more than a foot or two along here," he called back. "Been a wet winter down south, though, Barrett said. Folks headed to Independence might hit swollen creeks."

I didn't want to think about that. The clip-clopping of the horses' hooves, the sunlight on the world of grass, Hiram talking about weather farther south, nothing seemed quite real to me except the creek just ahead. I touched the Mustang's neck again. His head was still high, his ears stiffly forward.

"I'll wade," I called to Hiram.

"Fine with me," he called back. "I'll get the team across first. You wait on this side until I can get down to help if you need it."

As he said it, the road began to slope downward. I eased the Mustang a little by slowing my own pace. The wagon rolled on ahead of us, the gap widening gradually. As the sound of the wheels grinding against the gritty road lessened, I could hear the creek.

The Mustang lifted his head and tossed his mane. He nickered, and I patted his neck, talking to him. Then one of the wagon team mares whinnied, and I realized something. The Mustang did like me, and he did trust me. But he was following the horses.

"Slow up!" I shouted to Hiram.

He reined in and turned around on the driver's bench.

"It scares him to get separated from the mares."

Hiram nodded. "He's used to a herd."

The Mustang tossed his head so high that it pulled me off my feet for an instant. "I think I should sit on the wagon gate, after all, Hiram."

"I'll hold 'em still," he promised.

I loosened the lead rope and quickened my step until we were right behind the wagon again. I scrambled over the wagon gate and braced myself. "Start slow, please."

"You shout, we'll stop," Hiram said.

I held the lead rope as tightly as I could. The Mustang came forward at the first tug, and he kept up as the wagon rolled toward the creek. I let out a little slack when I heard the team wading in so the Mustang would be able to lower his head and pick his way.

At the water's edge he balked, and my arms were jerked out straight. Then he crow-hopped forward, catching up in one leap. I heard Hiram say something, but I couldn't understand him over the splashing.

"We're fine!" I called, figuring that was what he wanted to know. And we were fine. The Mustang wasn't a bit scared of the water, I could tell. He followed the wagon up the far bank without pulling the rope even once more.

"Maybe this'll work after all," Hiram called back to me. "I had my doubts."

I scrambled down from the wagon gate and reached out to pat the Mustang's forehead. The sun was bright overhead, and the day was silent except for the wagon wheels and the sound of the wind in the grass. It was strange to be so scared and so happy, all at once.

CHAPTER TWO

❨ ❨ ❨

*I did not mind walking with the small one holding
the rope. I knew I could pull it free if I needed to. But
I didn't. She never led me into danger.*

few days later, we saw other people on the
road ahead of us. They had oxen, and we
passed them about noon.

The men touched their hats, and I saw a girl
about my age peeking out of the wagon bed. I waved
at her, but she ducked back down like I had shouted
something mean at her. I wondered why.

"Maybe they're Mormon folks," Hiram said.

I took long steps to catch up. The Mustang stayed
beside me. "Why would that make her so shy and
scaredy?"

"There's been some kind of trouble. I don't know what it's all about, but they're mostly leaving the United States and going westward across the great desert, from what I've heard. No one seems to know where they are headed."

"What's Mormon mean?" I asked this time.

"It's their religion. People say some of them were shot over it back in Illinois or somewhere. They want to get away far enough to live in peace and build their own church, I expect."

"They don't look any different than the Methodists back home," I said.

Hiram laughed.

I scuffed a foot in the dust. "You know what I mean."

He nodded. "I do. People all want the same— enough to eat, their families safe, their faith and their opinions respected. I was raised a Presbyterian."

I stared at him. I had never known a Presbyterian. Or a Mormon. It was clear that the world was full of people and things I knew nothing about. It scared me a little, to think that.

Hiram looked at me sidelong and smiled. "I am glad, so far, that I decided to leave. You?"

I smiled back at him. "Oh, yes. I hated Mr. and Mrs...." I trailed off because it sounded too disrespectful. It was the kind of thing my own father would have punished me for.

"I apologize," I said.

He didn't answer. He looked straight ahead at the road for a while. The Mustang tugged at his lead rope, and I turned to pat his neck and scratch his jaw beneath the halter.

"I didn't like them either," Hiram said quietly. "But they fed you, and they paid me fair and let me use the shed. I had nowhere else."

I pulled gently at the Mustang's forelock, and he tossed his head. "I didn't either."

"So we should just be grateful," he said.

I nodded. "But we are glad we left," I said, hoping it would make him smile. It did.

"We are," he agreed. He gestured at the Mustang. "So is he."

I patted the Mustang's neck. "He surely is."

Hiram glanced at me. "I wish he could talk. Then he could tell us about the country we'll be crossing."

The Mustang tossed his head to drive off a biting

fly. It looked like he was nodding. I grinned, and Hiram laughed.

I dropped back and looked into the wagon bed as we walked. Hiram had brought two iron pots and a coffee pan. He had ten tins of biscuits and some salt pork, as well as twenty pounds of beans and some oats. He had bought a box of last year's apples from Mr. Svensen—a neighbor who had planted ten apple trees not far from my parents' old place. The root-cellar apples were nearly gone, and the biscuits were thinning out fast.

He looked back and saw me looking at the food stores.

"We'll buy more as we go along," he told me. "I saved up most of my wages—didn't cost me anything living in that pig shed and eating at Mrs. Stevens's table."

The nights were still cold. Hiram loaned me one of his blankets the first night, and he told me to keep it. We formed habits as we went. I slept in the wagon bed, and he slept beneath it, with a folded tarp between him and the damp ground.

From the second night onward, Hiram hobbled the wagon team every night instead of tethering them. The mares were good at the crabbed, short-ened stride the hobbles forced them to use. With the soft cotton rope loosely tying their front legs together, they could wander and graze; they just couldn't gallop.

At night, the Mustang was tethered on a long rope tied to an iron stake Hiram drove into the ground with a heavy mallet. The first few nights I had lain awake, worried and listening, but the Mustang tolerated the staking rope until it began to get light—or until the mares wandered too far away. Then he snorted and paced in a circle until I woke.

Shivering out from beneath my blanket, I un-tied the tether line to walk him closer so he could graze with the mares. Then I'd lead him back to the stake, slowly, pausing for him to graze, and the mares would follow.

I wished the Mustang could be free to move around, too, but I was afraid to try hobbling him. I rarely tried to touch him anywhere but his head and his neck. When I did, he shied away from me. I was certain he wouldn't let me touch his legs, much less fasten rope hobbles around his pasterns.

One morning a whistle behind us made Hiram and me both turn. A group of heavy wagons was coming up behind us. Hiram pulled the team off the rutted road and reined them in. I followed, leading the Mustang.

"Better to let them go past," Hiram said. "I don't want to push the mares to stay ahead of them."

I watched the people approaching. The men were whipping up the horses, keeping them at a smart trot in spite of the heavy-looking wagons. They had twenty or so spare horses running loose, herded along by young men riding saddle mounts.

They looked like one family, all sandy-haired and dark-eyed. The girls were pretty. A few of them waved, and I waved back, wondering if we would see any of them at Council Bluff.

One of their wagons was the oddest-looking rig I had ever seen, shaped like a boat and made out of leather. I wanted to ask them about it, but no one paused to talk—they were all walking fast to keep up with the wagons.

"How far is it to Oregon?" I asked Hiram once they had passed us.

"Over two thousand miles."

I turned, astonished. "That far?"

He nodded.

"What will we do without more horses?" I asked him. "What if one goes lame or gets away from us?"

"I think we should use oxen," he said as we got ourselves back onto the rutted road.

I began to think about all the things that could go wrong on a journey that long—or as best as I could imagine it. The wagon wasn't very big or anything near as stout as what Mr. Barrett had recommended. I was silent so long that Hiram began to whistle a tune, very softly, in time to the mares' hoofbeats. After a while had passed, he turned and looked at me. "People say there are animals for sale from people deciding at the last moment not to go, having to turn back, all kinds of reasons."

I opened my mouth, meaning to tell him that I would work hard to earn my keep, but that wasn't what came out. What I said was this: "Two thousand miles?"

Hiram didn't answer. He just pulled his hat a little lower on his forehead and settled himself on the wagon seat.

❧ ❧ ❧

Two days later Hiram bought us each a winter coat and a hat in a dry goods emporium in a little town called Des Moines. There were notices pinned up outside about Iowa becoming a state. I stared at them. My parents had signed petitions for statehood. They had wanted Iowa to be part of the United States.

"Is Oregon a state?" I asked Hiram as he led the way up the street toward a grocer's sign. He shook his head.

"No. It was French because of the trappers out there. Now it's English territory, but no one really has hold of it yet. That's the biggest reason people are going. The farmland is all there for the taking."

I thought about what he had said as we got dried beans and flour and a bag of potatoes from a man in a dark little grocer's built onto the side of a livery stable.

After that, the Mustang was restless, so I stayed outside by the wagon while Hiram talked to a butcher across the street. The man had a deep voice that boomed out the doorway, and I overheard him talking about the bad winter they'd had, how the ground still wasn't warmed up and farmers weren't selling off hogs cheap. All this was to make sure that Hiram knew what a bargain he was getting.

I stood close to the Mustang, glaring at two boys who seemed fascinated by him. One held a rock in his hand, loosely, as though he always carried a rock, just in case he needed it. I wondered if there were a lot of snakes here. Or wolves. Or maybe other boys made fun of him. His ears were big and stuck out from his head a little more than most, and his hair looked like sun-bleached straw.

A farm wagon rolled past, and the Mustang whinnied to the horses. They answered him, and the farmer popped his whip above their backs to remind them of their work.

"Barrett said a man should take two hundred fifty pounds of bacon for every adult in his party and half that for each child," Hiram grunted as he lifted the last of six paper-wrapped parcels into the wagon. "We have nearly that much now."

"Mr. Barrett talked about water barrels, too," I said, remembering.

Hiram nodded. "Yes. And medicines and spare clothing and two extra pairs of shoes and—"

"Do you have enough money for all that?" I asked him.

He shook his head, then tapped one finger against his temple. "Not enough. But what I have is better than money. I can always barter work if need be."

The Mustang shifted uneasily, and I looked up to see the two boys had come back. They had brought friends, so now there were four of them. The original two stood up front; their friends hung back, watching.

Hiram followed my glance. "Do you boys have business with us?" he asked politely.

The boy with the rock didn't answer, but the other one did. "No sir, just looking at your horse. We never seen one that color."

"Please stand back a little farther, gents," Hiram requested, his voice mild. The boys in back sidled down the boardwalk. The other two didn't move. "He is a wild horse," Hiram told them. "He is dangerous."

The boy with the rock hefted it in his hand.

"That's hard to believe. I've seen lots bigger horses."

Hiram took a step toward them, and they took a step back. "I startled him once. His hoof struck the stall planks here." Hiram patted an imaginary wall a few inches from his head.

I stared, wondering if he had ever told Mr. Stevens.

"If he's that mean, he should be shot," the boy with the rock said.

I tried to catch Hiram's eye, but I couldn't. I didn't want these boys standing so close, talking like this. The one with the rock worried me.

"He's wild," Hiram said, "not mean. He loves the girl. The rest of us had better stay back and be careful."

"How'd she get a wild horse?" one of the boys asked.

Hiram didn't answer. He turned and bent to the task of straightening up the wagon so the bundles of salt bacon got their own place on the lowest layer. I could smell it. It wasn't all that fresh. It still made my mouth water. We'd had plain beans and biscuits for a long time.

Hiram began to whistle. All eyes shifted to me.

"He's a Mustang," I said, not knowing what else to say to them.

"From out west?" said a boy who hadn't spoken a word yet. He wasn't so hard and snippy as the boy with the rock. He sounded like he was really interested.

I nodded. "That's where we're going," I said. "Oregon."

"Just you and your pa?" the one with the rock demanded. "You'll never make it."

The nicer boy elbowed him. "Don't mind Grover. His family is talking about going, and he doesn't want to."

I had no idea what to say, so I didn't say anything. I just wanted them to go away and leave us alone.

"What did you name the Mustang?" the nicer boy asked me.

I was quiet again because I hadn't even thought about naming the Mustang—not once. It didn't seem like he needed a name. He wasn't really mine—or anyone else's.

"Who cares what some girl names her horse," the boy with the rock said. Then he pivoted on one heel and turned, whipping a side-arm throw so hard that the stone knocked a chip out of a barrel in front of the dry goods store across the street. "I don't mind going," he said, turning back. "I just hate leaving."

His friends laughed, but it made perfect sense to me. I felt the same way. I didn't want to go back to the Stevenses, ever. But I would almost certainly never see my family's graves again, or anyone I knew. The thought scared me.

I tried to catch his eye, but he was already walking back and forth, toeing the dust, looking for another stone.

"Katie?" Hiram said from the driver's bench.

"I'm ready," I said over my shoulder.

Hiram clucked at the team, and they started off.

I walked the Mustang after the wagon, glancing back every few seconds.

I saw the blond boy find another stone. He hefted it, then tossed it a few times, settling it into his hand. He waited until we were almost out of range, then he threw it. It hit close, sending up a little puff of dirt a foot away from the Mustang's heels.

He danced sideways, half rearing, as he always did when something startled him. I jumped to one side and let out the long lead rope, letting him react to the unexpected spatter of sand that had come from nowhere. Only once he quieted and I was sure I had a good hold of him did I turn to glare at the boy.

He was laughing, half doubled over, and for an instant I hated him. There was no point in shouting an insult. The boy wouldn't care, and it might startle the Mustang again. So I just walked after the wagon with my back straight and my shoulders squared—but I was *furious*. What kind of boy would do such a thing? What if the Mustang had broken free, or I had gotten tangled in the rope and he had dragged me?

That night, the Mustang woke me even earlier than usual with his whuffling and pacing. I sighed and rubbed my eyes and got up in the dawn dusk. It was chilly, and I shivered into my shoes, then pulled on my new coat.

I slid out of the wagon bed, trying not to make the springs creak, and went to untie the tether rope. It wasn't light enough out to see my breath, but I knew it soon would be.

The instant the line loosened, the Mustang took off at a trot, headed toward the mares, pulling me along. I ran with him, half awake. "Slow down," I whispered, laughing a little at how eager he was. Then, all in an instant, I stumbled over a hassock of prairie grass and sprawled on the ground. The air went out of my lungs in a whoosh, and for a second I lay still, unable to believe it had happened. I heard the hissing sound of the long tether line, dragging through the grass—then the hoofbeats of the Mustang, free at last, breaking into a gallop.

I scrambled to my feet and stood, shaking, unable to do anything but watch as he galloped straight past the mares and pounded off into the near dark until I could no longer see him at all. His hoofbeats faded to silence. I sank to my knees and pounded my fists on the ground. How could I have been so stupid? How could I have just let go of the rope like that?

I fought tears as I got back to my feet. I would go after him. I could ride one of the mares bareback. We didn't have a bridle, but I could use the head-stall from the harness and knot the reins shorter.

I turned and ran toward the wagon. I would

have to wake Hiram, then get the harness bridle on one of the mares. By the time I was mounted, the Mustang would be miles away in the dawn dusk. In what direction? By the time it was light enough to see, he would be long gone. But Hiram would understand. I couldn't just let him go like this. I *couldn't*.

One of the mares nickered, and I slowed, turning, listening, afraid to hope. The mare nickered again. Then I heard the faint sound of hoofbeats—getting louder.

I stared into the gray light, hoping, my hands clasped together, as the Mustang galloped back into sight. He leaned into a long, sloping turn that brought him past me, then he slowed and veered toward the mares. He slid to a stop beside them and pranced in a circle.

I started toward him. "Stand easy," I murmured over and over. "Stand easy. I won't hurt you; you know that."

He was wary. Every time he moved away from me, I stopped. Finally, he dropped his head to graze. I approached him, talking quietly. He let me walk up and put my hand on his neck, then reach down to pick up the rope. I slowly gathered it into a coil. I was so grateful that he had come back that my knees felt weak.

"If you leave, who will I talk to?" I asked him, knowing that anyone who heard me talking to a horse like this would think I was touched. But it was true. I had no family anymore. Hiram was very kind to me, but he was not my father. "I don't want to be alone," I whispered, and the Mustang lowered his head and touched my cheek, his breath still coming fast from the gallop. "I am so scared to be all alone," I breathed. And I held on to the Mustang's mane and let myself cry hard—exactly the way I had back in the Stevenses' barn.

The Mustang did what he had done then. He stood still and let me lean against him. He was motionless for a long time, his head up, breathing in the scented air of dawn, touching the top of my head with his muzzle. When I stepped back, he began to graze again.

CHAPTER THREE

❧ ❧ ❧

There are many kinds of two-leggeds.
Some mean no harm. Others seem to mean nothing
else. It was wonderful to run free, but the scent of the
mares and the small one brought me back. I do not
want to be alone in a land of two-leggeds.

*T*he next night, I stood holding the tether
line, letting the Mustang graze next to the
mares as long as I could stay awake, then I tethered
him near them—instead of near the wagon. I woke
up worried, but he was still there, grazing peacefully with the wagon team.

"It's natural for a stallion to want a band of
mares," Hiram said that morning. "Mares and a
batch of healthy foals to protect."

Four nights later, I didn't tether the Mustang at
all. I stayed awake, watching him sleep next to the

mares. Three or four times there was some little sound, a rustling in the grass or an owl dropping down to catch a mouse.

The Mustang would open his eyes as though he hadn't been asleep at all. His head would lift, and he'd wait, listening and watching and scenting the night air. Then, when he was sure there was no danger, he would close his eyes again. Now that he had mares to watch over and protect, the Mustang was calmer. I didn't take his halter off because I was afraid he might not let me put it back on, but I untied the lead line. And every morning after that, he let me walk up to him while he stood calmly and tie it on again.

Twice we had to ford rivers. The Mustang followed the wagon across, steady even when the water was deep. The horses all had to swim a little way to get over the second one. The wagon slewed with the current, and Hiram shouted at me to hang on. For a long instant, I thought we were going to wash downstream, then the horses' hooves touched the bottom again, and the wheels began to turn. Hiram guided them up the muddy bank, keeping to the rutted tracks of wagons that had come before us.

"Too close," he said to me on the far side. "Far too close to calamity for me."

I jumped down from the wagon gate, my skirt soaked, my knees like rubber. We camped early and spread out our possessions and provisions on the grass to dry overnight.

A few days after the second river crossing, we saw another group of wagons behind us. The day after that, there were wagons behind us and in front of us. It made the Mustang skittish, but not as much as I had feared. He was getting used to the sound and sight of people more than he ever could have locked away in a barn. When he was most nervous, he would walk right next to me, so close that I could feel his breath on my neck.

One evening, we couldn't find a place to camp that was out of earshot of the other wagons. The Mustang jittered all night long. He tried to watch all the strangers, tried to hear every footstep, every voice, turning and shifting his weight, pawing at the ground. It scared me. If something startled him when he was that uneasy...

If he attacked anyone, someone *would* shoot him, and there would be little I could do about it. When other wagons were close, I stayed near him and warned people away if anyone tried to approach him. I stayed awake late enough to know that no one would come close to the mares—and I got up early enough to get him back on the lead rope before other camps were up and stirring.

I began to think that we should stay away from Council Bluff and anywhere else that was crowded—maybe we could set out alone and join a wagon train once we were away from the crowds.

I explained all that to Hiram one evening. "He's calmer than he was," I said. "But maybe not calm enough to walk through a crowd."

"Well, no one will ever mistake him for a farm horse," Hiram answered.

I knew he was right. Other horses looked sleepy and lazy next to the Mustang. He was always alert, always listening and watching. I looked up at Hiram. "Do you think we could strike off a little to the north or to the south and miss the worst of the crowds?"

He was silent. I had expected him to agree. When he didn't, I just waited, unsure what else to say.

"How are we going to cross the Missouri?" Hiram

asked finally. His voice was gentle. "The ferries operate where the crowds are."

"Can't we find a ford like we did with the other rivers?"

He shook his head. "The Missouri is a mile or two wide, Katie."

A river a mile or more wide? I pulled in a long breath. I had no answer for that.

The next morning it started raining, a cold miserable rain. Hiram and I wore our new woolen hats—and they soaked through in an hour. The Mustang plodded along like a plow horse, and the mares walked with their muzzles nearly on the ground. Hiram and I barely spoke. I sat in the wagon by the gate, leading the Mustang along, my hands so cold that I kept fumbling the rope, almost dropping it more than once. I finally looped it around my wrist.

We came upon a slough that had standing water in it. Hiram reined in the mares. He got down out of the wagon and stood beside the swampy hollow.

Rain dripping off my nose, I blinked to squeeze the water out of my eyes and looked around. The rain had filled a long, shallow depression in the ground with water. I couldn't see the end of it in either direction.

Hiram set the brake and had me get down out of the wagon. "Get that rope off your wrist," he scolded. "What if he bolted?"

I nodded, feeling foolish, my teeth chattering.

"Stay here," Hiram said. "Keep the mares on the road. I'm going to walk that way and see if I can find the end of it."

I was too shivery-chattery to answer, so I nodded again and watched him go. The Mustang stood quietly beside me, and I could feel warmth rising from his sodden coat. I put my hands beneath his mane and leaned close. He didn't seem to mind, and I was grateful. In a few minutes, my shivers had calmed a little.

"I wish we could just be somewhere warm and dry tonight," I told the Mustang. He arched his neck and shook the water out of his mane. I stood close again, trying to keep warm.

He lifted his head sharply. I looked past him and saw a group of the big, arch-topped Conestoga wagons sliding and jolting down the track. They came slowly, the oxen picking their way through the muddy ruts. I kept hoping Hiram would turn around and come back before they got too near, but he didn't.

"You alone?" a man called out once they were in earshot.

I shook my head and pointed. "Mr. Weiss went that way, trying to find a route around the slough."

The man reined in his horses and climbed down. His wagon had a rounded canvas top. It was a prairie schooner, I was sure. I had never seen one, but Mr. Barrett had described them clear enough.

"You need a canvas hat," he said, walking toward me. I put myself between him and the Mustang.

"I'll have to get one before we start west," I said. My teeth were chattering again, and I clamped them shut. I didn't want him to feel sorry for me.

"Here comes your pa," he said, gesturing. I could just see a vague shape that had to be Hiram starting back toward me, stumbling and sliding in the deep mud.

"My guess is he didn't find a way around the slough, and I am inclined to take his word for it, even from here. Our wagons are heavier than yours anyway. I think we'll camp back there a ways until the rain stops at least."

He pointed at the Mustang. "Where'd that horse come from? He some kind of special breed?"

The question caught me off guard. He stepped forward, and I positioned myself in front of him. "He's a Mustang," I said. "He's pretty skittish still."

"A Mustang? Really? This far east?"

I nodded.

"You don't want to sell him, do you?"

"No," I said quickly.

The man smiled. "I'll ask your pa, but if that's how it is, I won't pester him. I can see you're attached to the animal. Tell him you're welcome to visit us and dry out for a while."

"Thank you kindly, sir," I said.

He turned and walked off, calling out for the others to get turned around and go back uphill to camp on higher ground. I counted. There were six wagons, six teams of eight oxen—and there were boys herding other stock out on the grass. I saw a milk cow and thought of Betsy. I hoped Mr. Stevens would sell her to the McCartys so she would have kind people to take care of her. She would love their little girls, especially if they brought her carrots from the garden.

I sighed, remembering the warmth of Mr. Stevens's barn. It took Hiram a long time to walk back. I stood shivering in the rain the whole time, watching the man and his party through the blurry curtain of the downpour as they set up their camp. There were children, all ages, I could see that much. I wanted more than anything to go up the hill and dry out beneath one of the tarps they were stringing up between the wagons. But I had to talk to Hiram and make sure of something first.

"Can't get around," Hiram called when he got close. He gestured up the hill. "They friendly?"

"They invited us to join their camp and wait out the rain," I said.

He wiped rain from his face and squinted at me. "That what you want to do?"

"Yes," I told him, "but he thinks you're my pa, and he wants to know if the Mustang is for sale."

Hiram grinned, rainwater running down his face across his teeth, it was raining that hard. "You told him not unless he wants to trade the whole state of Oregon?"

I didn't laugh. "I told him no, but he's going to ask you, too."

"Because he thinks I'm your pa."

"Yes."

Hiram wiped water off his face again. "You want him to think that?"

I hesitated. In a way, it'd be easier. The boys in Des Moines had assumed it. Probably just about everyone would. But it felt wrong. I had a pa, a wonderful, good pa. Just because the fever had taken him didn't mean I didn't have a pa.

"I'll tell him the horse stays with you, and you can think the rest of it through later, all right?" Hiram said. "They have tarps and tents it looks like, and covered wagons. Let's go visit long enough to get dry."

CHAPTER FOUR

❧ ❧ ❧

*The rain is cold. At least the mares are here to stand
beside. The little one and her companion seem even more
miserable than we are. Why do they not seek shelter?
Don't they know where the forests are? They must not.
The small one would take us if she knew.*

*W*e didn't even bother to hobble the mares.
They were standing with their heads so low I
knew they wouldn't even try to graze in the downpour.
They barely moved when we got the harness off. The
Mustang stood watch a little way off as always, peering
into the rain to make sure no danger was near. None
of them seemed to much notice our leaving.

Hiram and I walked up the hill, staying to the grass
beside the road to avoid sliding into the ruts—some
were three feet deep, running with the rainwater like
miniature rivers.

The man who had talked to me was Benton Kyler. He welcomed Hiram and me, then turned to a stout woman with the bluest eyes I had ever seen.

"Mary? We need hot coffee quick as anyone can get it. They're soaked through."

"Hiram Weiss," Hiram said, and put out his hand. Mr. Kyler shook it and led us to a tarp they'd strung up like an awning. The rainwater cascaded off the low end. There was an older man digging a trench to carry it away from the little shelter.

We came under the canvas. I was still cold and shivering, and my hair was soaked, but it was a pure delight to be out of the pouring rain. I blinked the rain out of my eyes and looked around. Everyone in the party was working at some chore.

Several young women were working to start a fire. They had made a little platform out of three flat rocks, and they were stacking kindling on them.

"You have any other clothes?" Mr. Kyler asked Hiram.

Hiram shrugged. "A few. Not enough to change just for being wet." He looked at me. "We'll have to get a tent."

Mr. Kyler was watching us closely. I could tell

he was wondering what we were doing with no tent, no covered wagon, our belongings adding up to less than half a small wagonload.

"We have plenty enough to share breakfast with you if you will join us," he said.

"I ought to tell you right off the horse is not for sale," Hiram said in a mild voice. I knew what he was doing, honest man that he was. If Mr. Kyler's hospitality was aimed at getting the Mustang, Hiram didn't want to accept it.

"I thought as much," Mr. Kyler said, "from your daughter's reaction." He took off his hat and slapped it against his thigh. Rainwater spattered. "I intend to ranch horses in Oregon," he added as he settled his hat. "If you decide to sell, I'd buy him."

Hiram nodded and cast me a look. "It'd be her decision."

Mr. Kyler raised his eyebrows.

Hiram shot me a second glance. Mr. Kyler was clearly surprised that Hiram didn't have final say over the Mustang. Hiram was wondering if we should set it straight about him not being my pa. If we were going to do it, now was the time.

I took a deep breath. "Hiram and I are traveling together because I'm an... because I'm... because I..." My voice stuck, and I couldn't force the word *orphan* out of my mouth. I had never said it before, aloud or in my thoughts, and it just lodged sideways and stuck.

"She lost her whole family in the fever up around Eldridge a few years back," Hiram explained for me. "A lot of Scott County families lost folks."

"I've heard that families all over Iowa and Illinois lost kin," Mr. Kyler said.

"It was the same in New York State," Hiram said. I turned to look at him. His voice had sounded heavy, sad.

Mr. Kyler adjusted his hat. "That where you're from?"

Hiram nodded, his face expressionless. "Grew up there."

I hadn't known that. I wondered what else had happened to him in New York.

"Here's your coffee," the woman sang out as she came toward us, ducking under the tarp.

The tin cups were hot enough to warm my hands. When I took the first sip, I tasted bitter coffee, but

I also tasted sugar! I glanced up and saw the woman looking at me.

"Thank you very kindly, ma'am."

She smiled. "Call me Mary."

I lowered my eyes. I was not used to calling adults by their given names. My pa would have been irritated with my calling Hiram anything but Mr. Weiss, even though he had been a hired hand at the Stevens farm all three years I had lived there and he wasn't all that old. Pa would be furious if I extended that familiarity to a complete stranger who wasn't hired help. I heard a soft, motherly chuckle, and I looked up.

"All right, you can call me Mrs. Kyler. But if you do, you'll get several different women answering every time you shout."

I took off my soaked hat and smiled at her. My mother had liked making jokes.

"And you are...?" she prompted me.

"I'm Katie Rose, and I apologize, ma'am," I said, ashamed of my manners. Then I remembered. "Mary," I added, but it felt wrong to call her that. "Mrs. Kyler," I tacked on. Then, like I couldn't manage to end the sentence, I said, "Ma'am."

I felt silly. I was shivering and nervous and half worried about the Mustang, and it felt like my mouth wanted to keep going, no matter how foolish I made myself sound.

Mrs. Kyler just laughed, the warm kind of laugh that says it is all right if you laugh, too. So I did. Then I took another long sip of the sweet coffee. The sharp smell of kindling smoke made me turn. The young women had a big cookfire going. I moved to stand closer, and no one seemed to mind.

There was another young woman with a baby in her lap, sitting on a wagon step at the edge of the tarp shelter. She was smiling, playing peekaboo. The baby was laughing, a sound like a clear, swift creek.

"I can have Annie find a dry dress for you," Mrs. Kyler said, gesturing to a fair-haired woman standing nearby. She looked eighteen or nineteen to me. "Annie's the only one we haven't married off, so she's the only one with time on her hands," Mrs. Kyler joked. Annie smiled good-naturedly, and I saw her glance at Hiram. He met her eyes for a second, then they both looked away.

Mrs. Kyler was still smiling at me, waiting for

an answer. I thought about it. A clean dress would be heavenly. It was noisy and comfortable beneath the tarps the Kylers had strung between their wagons. I could hear children laughing, a baby crying, and the sound of men's voices—all muted by the sound of the rain. It was a big family. Wash days must have included a mountain of soiled clothes for these women. "You are very kind," I said, "but I'll dry out fine, ma'am." I pressed my lips together. I was not going to stammer my way through calling her Mary and Mrs. Kyler and ma'am again, and I was not going to take favors I couldn't pay back. It was bad enough how much I had taken from Hiram.

Hiram came to stand beside me by the fire. Annie moved over to make room for him.

"You two are welcome to bed down here tonight," Mr. Kyler said. We'll find a dry spot for you some-wheres."

I looked at Hiram and shook my head, a tiny motion that I hoped no one else noticed. I couldn't leave the Mustang alone all night. All we had meant to do was visit long enough to dry out.

"We'll be fine," he said. "We'll bunk beneath the

wagon bed to stay dry if we have to." He looked out from beneath the tarp. "Rain will probably stop before long anyway."

Mr. Kyler walked over then, warming himself at the fire. I sipped at my coffee to avoid his eyes—and everyone else's. It was strange, being around so many people at once.

"What do you do for a living, Mr. Weiss?"

Hiram blew at his steaming coffee, then sipped it before he answered. "I was working as a plow hand. But I have other trades."

Mr. Kyler nodded without speaking and waited for Hiram to get another sip of the hot coffee.

Hiram winked at me, then looked at Mr. Kyler. "I can lay brick, build a dry stone wall; I'm a fair carpenter and a sawyer. I learned to shoe horses, and I am a fair hand at training them as well. I can dress leather and sew harness, and I'm a fair shot at hunt. I built boats with my father. I can swim like a fish. I am good with numbers. I can figure sums in my head, work percentages and so on. My pa was death on laziness. We worked the farm and went to school both."

I blinked, staring at him. I had never heard him

string together more than a dozen words at a time. Annie was smiling, looking as amazed as I felt.

"A good man to have around out west," Mr. Kyler said. Annie smiled wider.

I took a drink of coffee and kept glancing at Hiram as if I had just met him. He sounded like a one-man homestead builder. I wondered if Mr. Stevens had known he could do all those things. I surely hadn't.

"Do you have kin or friends to meet in Council Bluffs?" Mrs. Kyler asked Hiram.

He shook his head. "The girl and I had plans, but the other folks disappointed us both, so we struck out on our own."

"You ever been married?"

Hiram nodded. "I'm a widower, ma'am."

I stared at him again. I had suspected it, but he had never told me. I saw his eyes meet Annie's for a split second, and then he looked square at Mr. Kyler again.

"You intend to join a wagon party in Council Bluffs?" Annie asked.

Hiram nodded. "Thought we'd just meet a few folks and see who needed a farrier or a carpenter."

I listened, still amazed at how much Hiram was talking lately.

The noisy sizzle of bacon grease made me turn around so fast I nearly spilled my coffee. I guess my reaction looked funny because a girl with long dark braids made a face, and they all giggled. One of them was carrying a white cat. It was as relaxed as a doll in her arms.

I looked away from the skillet, blushing, wishing I hadn't seemed so greedy for food. I was wolfish hungry, but I didn't want to be a rude guest.

"You hoping to marry again?" Mrs. Kyler was asking Hiram.

"Mary!" her husband chided. "You'll run him off if you don't stop prying."

Hiram laughed easily. "I've never had better coffee and never wanted it worse. I'm not going anywhere just yet."

Mr. Kyler chuckled at that, and I glanced back at the girls. They were still staring at me. The girl with long dark braids leaned close to a tall girl to whisper.

I turned away quickly. I knew we might end up traveling with these folks, and I hated the idea of wondering what the Kyler girls were saying about me all the way to Oregon.

It stopped raining about half an hour later, and we walked back down the hill to hobble the mares and settle in. The ground was soaked, and Hiram made me sleep up in the wagon bed, laying our driest piece of canvas beneath his bedroll.

When the stars came out, they looked like ice scattered across the sky. I finally stopped shivering and slept.

CHAPTER FIVE

❦ ❦ ❦

How many of the two-leggeds are there?
Every day we see more of them. They do not attack, or
even approach too near. But they worry me. Out of so
many, there will be a few who are dangerous.

*I*t rained again before noon the next day. Then the sun came out, and the men walked the long slough, testing the bottom with long sticks.

I stayed with the Mustang, close to our wagon. He was grazing peacefully with the mares, but I was afraid to leave him alone with so many people around. A shout, a rifle shot at a rabbit in the grass, a baby screaming—anything might startle him.

I took the hobble off the mares, then kissed the Mustang's velvety muzzle and told him I knew he would protect them. By midmorning, some of the younger Kyler men had come down the hill to talk to Hiram. Mr. Kyler joined them, carrying his tin cup of coffee. None of their womenfolk had left the camp.

Hiram kept them all away from the Mustang, and I was grateful to him. I stood off to one side, listening.

"Every delay matters," Mr. Kyler kept saying.

"It can," Hiram agreed.

"Three days here could mean three days in snow-storms next fall in the Northwest Territory," one of the younger men put in. I had noticed him the night before, standing beside a woman so tiny she looked like a young girl.

Everyone was nodding. "Weather like that can kill a baby," another man said. I knew from the worry in his voice—he was the baby's father.

Hiram shaded his eyes, staring at the water still standing in the slough.

Mr. Kyler narrowed his eyes. "Hiram? You see a way to get us over it?"

Hiram was silent. He knelt and pushed his fingers into the matted grass. He straightened. "Do you have sod knives?"

Mr. Kyler nodded. "One of the books said we should bring them, so we did, even though we all intend to settle in timber country."

Hiram looked thoughtful. "It could take all day," he began. "But if we cut lengths of the sod and layered it in the shallowest place, the grass mat would support the wagons, I think."

I head a murmur of admiration go through the men. I smiled, remembering Hiram tapping his forehead.

"Let's get to it then, boys," Mr. Kyler said.

The younger men started back up the hill, talking among themselves.

"They all your sons?" Hiram asked him.

Mr. Kyler glanced at them. "Three are, Charles, Andrew, and Ralph. The other one is Henry, married to Christina, my daughter. We left three married daughters behind. Couldn't talk them into it. It about killed Mary to leave them."

Hiram stared off into the distance. I didn't know what he was thinking, but I could guess. He was wishing that his own wife had lived, that he had sons. I wished the same thing in my own way. I wanted my family back. One day it might have been like this one, big and friendly, with laughter around the campfires every night.

Hiram bent to poke at the tangled mat of prairie grass again, then straightened. "You are a fortunate man," he said quietly.

Mr. Kyler nodded awkwardly, concentrating on his coffee cup. Then he looked up. "We're jumping off at Council Bluff."

Hiram nodded. "As are we."

Mr. Kyler smiled. "May as well travel that far together, I suppose."

Hiram squinted into the sun. "I think tomorrow we'll hit the old Fort Kearny Road."

Mr. Kyler looked thoughtful. "I've been thinking we'd find it every day for a week. Ought to be soon."

Hiram turned away and spotted me for the first time. "Katie? Will you do your best at drying anything you can while we're at this?"

I nodded and started back down toward our wagon, feeling almost happy. Hiram *asked* me to do things, instead of telling me. He was kind and smart, and he would get us to Oregon. And there, I would find my uncle Jack one way or another, no matter how long it took.

As I spread out our blankets and tarps on the steaming prairie grass, I imagined doing the work with two or three cousins to help me. We would laugh and sing rounds to make the work go faster.

The sun got stronger as the day passed. The blankets were close to dry by the time the men had cut the wet sod and dragged the pieces into the slough, laying them on top of one another until they had built what amounted to a sod bridge.

Our wagon was lightest, so we went first.

The Mustang was so used to following the wagon that he barely hesitated, picking up his hooves like he was prancing in a pasture when he came to the soft sod. The mares were steady as always.

The Kylers burst into a cheer when we drove off the sod bridge and back onto the muddy road on the far side. Hiram pulled the mares to a halt and set the brake.

We watched the Kylers' wagons—all six of them—wobble and sway as they came across. Their oxen were far heavier than our horses, too, and they went more slowly, picking their way. The sod was rutted by the time the last wagon came over, but it held. We all cheered again.

Then we set off. Hiram and I went first, the horses being faster than the oxen—and our wagon so light. We bogged down midafternoon, and the Kyler men came plodding through the mud to push us free.

The Mustang shied as they came closer, and I led him off a little way. He stood with his head held high, his nostrils flared.

"It's all right," I told him over and over. "They're good people, they know you're mine. Hiram and I told them that." He snorted and circled, always coming back to face the wagon with the crowd of strangers shoving at the gate while the mares strained against the harness.

When the wheels finally came loose, there was a squelching sound and the mares stumbled forward, surprised when the wagon finally rolled free. Hiram drove them along a distance of a few rods, just far enough to be well clear of the softest mud, then he reined in and set the brake. He got out to knock the worst of the mud off the wheel hubs.

I walked the Mustang closer, ready to fall in behind the wagon when the Kylers left.

"He's a fine animal," one of the younger men called as they started the trek back through the mire to their own wagons. He stopped to look at the Mustang, shading his eyes from the slanting afternoon sun.

I nodded politely.

He took off his hat and slicked his hair back, then put it on again. "My pa says you aren't interested in selling him?"

"That's right," I called back.

"Is he fast?"

I didn't know what to say. "I've never raced him," I finally told him.

He started toward me, and I felt my stomach tighten. "Don't come another step," I said, raising my voice.

He stopped, looking puzzled. "I mean you no harm at all. I apologize if I've frightened you."

I shook my head. "Not me, the Mustang. He doesn't trust people."

"You're afraid to race him, then?"

I nodded, then I shook my head. "No one has ever ridden him that I know about. I don't think he'd stand for it."

He looked thoughtful. "My name is Andrew. I'm the youngest Kyler boy."

I almost laughed. He had a blond beard, and he looked like a grown man to me.

"Hannah is my wife. The one with little Rachel; she's our first baby."

I nodded. I remembered Hannah laughing and singing.

"We're just starting out," he said.

I nodded again, reaching out to pat the Mustang's neck. He was nervous, tossing his head. I had no idea why Andrew was telling me all about his family, but I wished he would move farther away.

"A stallion like that could build a good herd in a few years," he said wistfully—and then I understood his friendliness.

"He isn't for sale," I said quickly. "He'll never be for sale."

"What good is a horse you can't ride?" he asked politely.

"He isn't for sale, mister," I repeated, amazed at how rude and unfriendly I sounded.

Andrew Kyler nodded and doffed his hat. Then he walked away. I led the Mustang back to the wagon. Hiram watched me as we got close.

"He want to buy the stallion?"

I nodded.

"People have never seen anything like him. That won't be the last offer."

I heard an odd tone in his voice, and I turned to look at him squarely. My throat was tight. "You think I should sell him."

"Maybe you ought to consider it, if you meet someone you think would take good care of him," Hiram said. "He will never make a girl's mount— maybe not even a man's horse. He'll never pull a wagon."

"But Hiram..."

"Just think about it," he said. "You can't get a decent night's rest for guarding him, and you can't leave him even for a few minutes without worrying if he's going to hurt someone. This isn't like bringing a pet like the Kyler girls' white cat."

"He isn't for sale, Hiram," I said flatly, starting to feel angry with him. If anyone should understand how much the Mustang meant to me, it was Hiram.

Hiram turned to face the road. "All right, Katie," he said over his shoulder. "All right, then."

CHAPTER SIX

❦ ❦ ❦

The sky was open and wide, and the grass
was growing and endless. Somewhere under this sky
there were forests and meadows and the grasslands
I remembered. Not close, but... somewhere.

*L*ate one afternoon, we saw Council Bluff for
the first time. Hiram reined in and got down
off the wagon to look down at the Missouri River
and the town of Kanesville.

Mr. Kyler pointed. "Trader's Point is down that
way. Colonel Sarpy's new ferry is running a gold
mine business, we were told. Best get there early."

We made our camp. I did my chores, then led
the Mustang closer to the edge of the bluff and
stood in the twilight watching the light change the
color of the river below.

The Missouri ran between huge bluffs, and there were camps and settlements on both sides. The river was swift, muddy, and wider than I could have imagined. The sunset turned it the color of old copper.

The next morning, we all drove the wagons down the steep road into the town of Kanesville, the men pulling on the brake handles all the way down to keep the wagons from rolling too fast. The river seemed bigger with every step we took.

Hiram glanced back at the Kyler's first wagon. The oxen were plodding steadily toward us. "What do you think? You want to travel with them to Oregon?"

I nodded. I had thought about it. "I like them."

Hiram nodded. "So be it, then. We'll need more, of course. Barrett said any party under thirty wagons was too small."

"Thirty," I echoed, tightening my hand on the Mustang's lead rope. "How will we meet that many people?"

Hiram gestured at the sea of wagons and settlements below. "How can we avoid it?"

I bit at my lip.

"The Mustang will be all right," Hiram said.

"He's smart, and he isn't as wild as you think he is anymore. If you'd let people come closer—"

"I just don't want anyone to get hurt," I interrupted, surprised at how angry I felt at his telling me how to handle the Mustang.

Hiram reached out and brushed the top of my head with the palm of his hand the way he had done now and then when Mrs. Stevens had scolded me. "Are you sure it's the horse that's afraid?"

I looked at him. "What do you mean?"

Before he could answer, two of the Kyler girls came running up the road toward us. It was the one with dark braids and the taller, thin girl who was usually with her. They were both around my age, I was pretty sure.

Watching them, I realized that I didn't know their names. I walked the Mustang off to one side, then looked back. They told Hiram something, then ran back toward the Kylers' wagons.

"What are their names?" I asked Hiram once they were too far away to hear.

He nodded. "Julia with the braids. The other one is Polly. I'm not quite sure who their parents are yet. I think Julia belongs to Ralph and

Ellen. Ralph's the tall man with the black hat."
He shrugged. "Benton sent them. He wants to go
straight on downriver now, and get in line at the
ferry landing. I expect he's right."

Hiram got the mares moving, and I led the
Mustang back onto the road. The Kylers' wagons
made a long line when we all stopped to wait for
a turn on the ferry. There were fifteen or twenty
wagons lined up in front of us, and the sounds of
children and chickens and bawling oxen and voices
were scaring the Mustang.

I kept a tight hold on the lead rope and walked
him back and forth and up and down, then around
and back around.... He was so fidgety. I knew
that if I tried to make him stand still, he would
only get worse.

I was pretty nervous, too. The ferry was a creaking flatboat that held two wagons and a dozen or
so people at a time. The ferrymen had long poles,
and they shoved at the river bottom, moving the
ferry along until they hit the deepest water in the
middle of the river.

Once they got that far, two men on the far side
turned a crank that reeled in a long cable attached

to the front of the ferry and dragged it through the strong current in the middle of the river. They used the poles again once it was back in the shallows.

They just turned the whole process around to bring the ferry back. Mostly, it was empty coming back, but twice there were families with farm wagons on it. One group was dressed up like they were going to a wedding. The other family had a wagonload of provisions to sell.

People surrounded them as soon as they made it plain that they had goods for sale. I saw Hiram walking toward them, his step quick and sure.

I looked back out as the next two wagons on our side were moving up the ramp onto the deck of the ferry. The horses were tossing their heads, eyes circled in white, switching their tails. The rails around the ferry made it look like a stall—but no stall had ever shifted and swayed beneath their hooves before.

I walked the Mustang up the street again, trying to calm him down. Hiram was carrying an oaken water barrel when he met me coming back. "How's he doing?"

"I don't think he'll let me lead him onto the boat. Hiram, the farm horses look fit to come undone riding like that, with the boat swaying and bobbing beneath them."

"You ever been on a boat?"

I shook my head.

"Can you swim?"

I shook my head.

"You afraid?" he asked me.

I let out a long whooshing breath. "Maybe."

He smiled at me. "If you are, he will be. He trusts you. If you act like it's too dangerous, he'll believe you."

I looked at the Mustang. He was holding his head so high, I had to crane my neck. I reached up and touched his muzzle. The instant he felt my hand, he lowered his head and pushed his fore-head against my chest.

I glanced at Hiram.

"See? He's depending on you."

I scratched the Mustang's ears gently. "We've watched it go back and forth all morning," I told him. "Nothing has happened. We'll be fine."

Hiram hoisted the barrel to his shoulder and grinned at me. "Keep walking him—that will help. I want to buy whatever else I can before our turn comes up. Things are expensive here—but even worse on the other side, people say. I am glad we got the bacon in Des Moines at least. Katie?"

"What?"

"I'll teach you to swim. No reason why girls shouldn't know how to swim."

I nodded, then started back up the road. As I walked, the Mustang followed me closely, easily. I almost never had to tug at the rope anymore, I realized. He kept an eye on me, and if I changed direction, he did, too.

I knew Hiram was right. The Mustang was depending on me to take care of him in this jumble of wagons and people. I rested my hand on his neck as we walked.

On the way back down the road, I saw the Kylers sorting out their stock. Polly and Julia and some of the younger girls were standing still, side by side, on one side of the oxen to keep them from wandering, it looked like. There were two older boys helping Andrew and the other Kyler men move the horses slowly away from the line of wagons.

None of the girls smiled at me, though they all watched closely as I walked past on the road. I hadn't been too friendly with them, I knew. But it seemed like they had no use for me at all. I had heard the younger ones' names. There was a Mary May, probably named after her grandmother, and a Patience and a Hope. I knew this because their mothers were calling them constantly.

There were two or three more, too, little girls who stayed close to their parents. I didn't know their names except for Rachel, Andrew and Hannah's baby daughter.

I glanced back toward the ferry landing. Hiram had walked our wagon to one side. So the Kylers were going first. I exhaled slowly. It'd take two or three trips across just to carry their animals, I realized—they had twenty or thirty horses and a bunch of mules, and all the ox teams, too. And then their six wagons...

I felt my stomach loosen; it'd be hours before we went. I patted the Mustang and combed his mane with my fingers. I liked the idea of learning to swim. I couldn't think of a single girl I knew about who could—and not that many boys, either. I imagined walking up to my uncle Jack's door and meeting my cousins for the first time. I would tell them I knew how to swim in a careless way, like it was nothing at all.

"Katie?"

It was a shout. I turned and spotted Mr. Kyler, hands cupped around his mouth.

"Yes, sir?" I called back.

"Hiram says to tell you he wants to go over first load," he yelled.

"Yes, sir!" I shouted back, and my stomach tightened right back up as I started down the hill. I stared out at the river. The ferry was halfway back.

As I got closer, I saw Hiram climbing back up on the driver's bench. Our goods were neatly arranged in the back of the wagon. The mares were standing quietly, their hips sloped. They were both resting one back leg.

"Sorry to surprise you," Hiram said as I came closer. The man down at the ferry said prices are better once you get across—there are so many over there they compete with one another more."

He looked at me intently for a moment. "You be steady and he will."

The ferry was sliding toward the planked dock. The men poled it in fairly straight. It only took them

෴ 69 ෴

a minute or two to get it lined up with the ramp.

Hiram clucked at the mares, and the wagon wheels turned. I stepped forward, keeping our distance behind the wagon the same as it was when we were going down a road.

The mares balked a little, and I caught my breath, slowing the Mustang down. Then they set their hooves on the ramp and Hiram popped the whip once to let them know they had to do this, that he wouldn't let them argue about it.

The ferry sank a few inches under the weight of the wagon and the team, then bobbed up level again when the Mustang and I faced it. I forced myself to step right onto the planks, knowing that Hiram was right. If I hesitated, the Mustang would know how uneasy I was.

I followed the wagon just as we had been following it for weeks, and the Mustang followed me. I felt him hesitate for a second once his forehooves were on the swaying deck, but then he came forward, lifting his hooves high as though he was walking in a bog. When Hiram reined in the team, I stopped and held the Mustang steady. He stood still, his head high and his eyes flickering from the boatmen to the mares, then out over the brown water.

Hiram set the brake and climbed down to pat the mares as the ferrymen set their poles in the muddy bottom and pushed away from the shore.

The Mustang snorted and shook his mane when the boat began to move. I forced myself to sound calm as I talked to him and rubbed his neck with the palm of my hand. I tugged at his mane. He blew out a whuffling breath and switched his tail even though there weren't any flies to speak of.

"How long has this ferry been here, sir?" Hiram asked the men.

"Not long, sir," one of them called back without looking. "Colonel Sarpy got the cables set less than a year ago."

They were bending their backs now, poling in long glides that sent us farther from the bank every second. I looked at the surface of the water and saw shapes just beneath it. Fallen trees? Sunken ferryboats? The shapes slid past, and I couldn't see them anymore.

I felt the current pushing sideways at the boat as the water deepened beneath us. The Mustang felt it, too. He tossed his head, and I could feel him trembling. I reached to pat his neck, rubbing my hand hard against his coat.

"You fellas need a hand?" Hiram asked.

"You paid your three dollars," one of them answered, grinning. "You earned the ride, mister."

I caught my breath. "Three *dollars*?" I whispered, just loudly enough for Hiram to hear. For a few seconds I forgot about the endless brown water beneath us.

Hiram nodded. "Think what it'll cost the Kylers to come across. They charge more for bigger wagons, for each person afoot...."

I shook my head, unable to believe that anyone dared charge so much.

"People have to get across," Hiram said. "I think the Kyler boys might swim a lot of their stock over. I heard them talking about it. Some have done it, I guess."

A little bump against the bottom of the boat startled me. The Mustang threw his head high and backed up.

"Stand easy," I said in the calmest voice I could manage. "It's all right." I rubbed at his neck again, and, after a long moment, I felt his rigid muscles loosen a little.

"What was that?" I asked Hiram.

"Probably just a drowned tree washed down in some storm, waterlogged and sunk beneath the surface." He smiled at me and climbed back up. He pretended to be driving the team, his hands high, swaying back and forth like we were on a bumpy road.

I laughed; I couldn't help it.

"How's that wild horse of yours doing?" Hiram asked after a few more minutes had passed.

"Better," I said. "It was just that little jolt that spooked him."

"We're about halfway," Hiram said. "Just keep talking to him and don't get yourself worried. Look."

I glanced up to follow his gesture. He was pointing at the far shore.

"That's the beginning of everything, Katie. This is the first day of our journey west."

"I keep thinking that most people will start coming back," the ferryman said, overhearing us. "I half expect there to be a longer line on the west side than the east side every morning."

"Why?" Hiram asked him.

The man shrugged. "It all sounds too good. I don't see how it could be real. A man told me yesterday that a married couple can claim a square mile in Oregon. He said the land is rich and the timber is high. Is that true?"

"So they say. You should go," Hiram said. "You're young."

The ferryman shrugged. "My mother is a widow, and I'm the only one left to care for her."

I watched Hiram trying to think of something to say to that. He couldn't. Finally, he lifted his head and looked down stream.

"Katie?" He jutted his chin to the south. "The Kylers are putting their stock across. Horses and mules it looks like."

A long way down the river I could see a milling band of animals and four mounted men behind them whooping and slapping their hats against their legs, trying to herd them into the water. For a long moment, it looked like the stock was going to refuse to go, then the first horse plunged in.

"They'll lose a few," the ferryman said.

Hiram shook his head. "I don't think so."

I watched, holding my breath, hoping all the Kyler menfolk and their horses made it across without any accident.

The Mustang heard the distant whinnying and turned his head sharply, his ears straight up and his eyes wide.

"It's all right," I told him. His nostrils were wide and his breath was quick. "Just a few more minutes, and we'll be back on land," I promised.

"Could be worse," Hiram said gently, and it took me a second to realize he was talking to the Mustang, not to me. "Could be much worse. At least this time you're headed back west."

I patted the Mustang's neck and held tight to the lead rope. There was a jolt when the cable stopped pulling and the men picked up their poles again.

"Stand easy," I told the Mustang. "We're almost there."

I kept looking downriver at the Kylers—they had picked a narrower place—but that meant the water was deeper. The horses were really drifting downstream as they swam.

Hiram was watching me, and when I looked up, he pointed back at the far shore. I turned, looking straight across, and caught my breath. We had drifted a long ways, too, in spite of the cables.

The ferry scraped over another submerged log or something; it was hard enough to really shake the boat hard this time. The Mustang reared reflexively, just barely lifting his front hooves from the planks, then settling again. He shook his mane and fixed his eyes on the shore. I patted him and talked quietly, willing the ferrymen to pole faster. Finally, finally, the ferry bumped against the dock, and the ferrymen let down the rails.

Hiram shook the reins and the mares stepped forward slowly as though they didn't quite trust the planks to hold them. The Mustang clattered forward, pulling me along. Once he felt soft earth beneath his hooves again, he slowed, turning his head to make sure I was all right. I looked back across the river. The brown water slid past, endless and quiet. It looked even wider from this side.

When I looked forward again, Hiram was gesturing at the sea of shacks, wagons, and tents. "I want to sell the mares and buy oxen," he said over his shoulder, raising his voice so I could hear him. "People say horses can't pull the weight and live on the prairie grass near as well as the work cattle can."

I hesitated, then nodded. I was fond of the mares, and the Mustang would hate it if they were gone, but I knew Hiram was probably right. "You all right?" Hiram called from the wagon.

"Fine!" I shouted back.

But it wasn't quite true. I was scared. Something about crossing the river had made it all much more real to me. We were setting off into a wilderness. "Two thousand miles," I whispered to myself.

CHAPTER SEVEN

✖ ✖ ✖

The small one led me across the wide river in a
way no horse could ever manage alone. The mares are so
calm about the two-leggeds' ways. I will never be.

By late afternoon the Kylers' wagons were safely
across and their stock had been regathered on
the west side of the river. In our first hour on the
west shore of the Missouri River, Hiram bought a
little tent, more provisions, a saw, and two beautiful splotch-colored oxen—but no one wanted to
buy our mares.

Hundreds of horses had been sold here already—
and sold cheap. A lot of people who crossed every
morning were selling wagon teams and buying oxen
or mules.

The oxen *were* beautiful, if such a heavy animal can be thought of that way. They were Ayrshires, Hiram had been told, from the farm of a man named Mr. James Brodie of Rural Hill, New York. They were an uncommon breed.

"The man said they are livelier than most kinds of work cattle, and stronger," Hiram said. "He sold them to me instead of another man because I promised I'd either keep them or find them a kind, careful owner once I got to Oregon."

I nodded, staring at the pair of huge beasts.

"He says they weigh around two thousand pounds apiece," Hiram told me.

I smiled. "Two thousand miles, two thousand pounds."

Hiram laughed.

That evening, while I sat and read my mother's book by firelight, Hiram sought out Andrew Kyler and came back with enough money to buy us spare shoes, more blankets, and a number of other things we needed.

"He bought both mares," Hiram told me. "He'll herd them all day and the stallion, too, if you want," Hiram explained. "You can go catch them up every evening and bring them back to the wagon so the Mustang won't have to be hobbled or tethered at night."

I let out a relieved breath and grinned at him. This was the best possible solution and one I had never expected. "Andrew Kyler is a good-hearted man," I said fervently.

Hiram chuckled. "Andrew Kyler is hoping the Mustang will take a mare to mate and she'll have a foal next spring."

"Oh." I blushed, feeling slow-witted not to have figured that out for myself.

Hiram reached out to pat my head. "We'll get mares once we're in Oregon, and you can raise a few colts yourself if you want to. I'll teach you what I know about horse training, but you can learn even more from the Kylers. Annie Kyler told me that her brother is the best horseman she's ever seen."

Hiram was smiling. "Annie is quite a horse-woman herself, her father says."

I smiled back at him, thinking about it. He liked Annie a lot, I could tell—he liked all the Kylers. Maybe he envied their big happy family the way I did.

What if Hiram and I could have a horse ranch

somewhere near them? The Mustang would sire beautiful colts. I would grow up to be a lady horse trainer. No one would believe it until they saw my beautiful horses.

It was so much fun to imagine it, to pretend it could come true. I laid down on my pallet that night, daring to imagine a horse ranch of my own. I knew it was impossible. Who ever heard of a girl owning anything? It was against the law, I was pretty sure. No woman I had ever heard of owned land or anything else. I sighed. Maybe my uncle Jack would want to raise horses....

In the morning, the menfolk went off for a few hours. I took a long time packing the provisions Hiram had bought, wrapping the flour in tight-woven canvas to keep the meal moths from laying their eggs in it. I made sure the top of the water barrel was greased and tight to keep the trail dust out. Then I brushed the Mustang—he still didn't like the feel of the currycomb, but he stood for it.

I finally fed the oxen a little dried corn so they would start to like me. They had sweet breath and mile-deep eyes, and they reminded me of Betsy, except for their size—and their color. I had never seen any kind of cow with such splashy-looking blotches of white and brown.

The Mustang was wary of them being so close.

"Do they remind you of buffalo?" I asked him. "Mr. Barrett said buffalo herds make the ground shake when they stampede. Is that so?"

I patted his neck, reaching beneath his mane to thread my fingers through the long coarse hair on the crest of his neck. I wished he could talk to me. Some people thought that buffalo weren't real—or at least that the stories people told about them were exaggerated.

"Katie!"

I looked up. Hiram was almost running toward me, his face full of excitement. "Mr. Kyler's found a good guide, I think."

I listened, feeling breathless, as Hiram told me about Mr. Wilkins. Like a lot of the guides, he had been a trapper. He had been west three times with groups of wagons, and he seemed to know a lot about the different routes and shortcuts. "He seems very sensible," Hiram explained. "Mr. Kyler ran across him. He listened a while, then rounded up the rest of us to hear him out. There'll be just twenty wagons in the party, counting us, if we go."

"How many wagons?" I asked him.

Hiram looked thoughtful. "Wilkins likes a smaller party. He says everyone has a few problems somewhere along the way, and the bigger the party, the more chance of bad delays. It makes sense, I guess. They leave in the morning."

I had been listening intently, but when he said we'd be leaving the next day, I caught my breath. Hiram didn't notice.

He slapped dust from his hat. "I'll find salt today and dried apples, if I can, and more canvas to make a wagon top for rain—and a canvas hat for you. People say to save back money to pay for restocking and blacksmith work and whatnot at the forts as we go. Things are even more expensive there."

He was talking fast, and it struck me how much he had changed. He smiled more now, and I had heard him whistling when he went back and forth to the Kylers' wagons.

"You worried?" he asked me.

I shrugged. "Do you think we'll make it all right?"

He nodded and patted my head. "We're both pretty tough, and the Mustang is tougher than both of us put together. We'll do."

I smiled at him. "You never used to talk this much."

He ducked his head, then looked at me. "I lost my family the same as you did, Katie."

I flushed, knowing I had been rude to say what I did. I started to apologize, but he stopped me.

"No. You're right. I didn't talk much for a few years. I'm feeling some better now. I nearly talked Annie to sleep last night."

"I am a little better, too," I said quietly. "Some of the time, anyway."

"Maybe some of the time is all we'll ever get," he said.

I nodded. "That'd be all right with me."

He grinned. "You'll be in love someday, Katie."

"Maybe you will, too," I said.

I waited for him to answer, but he didn't. I blushed, realizing I had probably offended him. A girl talking to a grown man about such things! "Sometimes I wonder what my life will be like," I said awkwardly, to fill the silence.

"You'll do fine wherever you go, Katie. You have a good heart and a stiff spine."

He took a few coins out of his pocket. "I'll stay with the Mustang for a while. Go look around and buy anything you think you might need."

I stared at him. "Just go off and...?"

He was nodding. "Buy what you'll need that I won't think of. Clothes and whatnot. Stretch the money. Give it some thought."

I took the coins and handed him the Mustang's lead rope. The stallion was completely calm now, standing quietly with the mares beside the wagon. The mares were nosing at the tattered grass beneath the wagon.

"He's used to me," Hiram said. "And he's had to get used to all this." He gestured, taking in the milling crowds and the hundreds of wagons.

"Where?" I asked vaguely, absorbed in my own nervousness about leaving the Mustang.

Hiram understood me, by some miracle.

He pointed. "Most are up that way. There are folks selling goods off tarps and blankets all along that side, and tents up the rise as well. Buy clothing too big. You'll grow this next year. Get sturdy goods, stout enough to take being washed on creek rocks instead of in a tub."

I glanced at the lead rope in his hand. It hung in a loose arc to the Mustang's halter. The stallion was half asleep, stamping a hoof now and then to scare off a biting fly.

"Go on," Hiram said.

"I won't be long," I promised.

"Take the time you need to take. I'll go over the wagon once more, see that everything is sound and ready."

I nodded and turned to walk away. It felt strange to leave the Mustang with Hiram in such a crowded place. But I knew that he was right. Even when the Mustang got startled and nervous now, he knew enough to settle down quick enough.

I glanced back and ran into a boy carrying a mound of tangled harness. I apologized and walked on, blushing fiercely.

Hiram was right. There were so many selling goods that I didn't know where to start.

Some of the sellers lived in tents pitched in long rows. Some had pulled their wagons into the line. There were a few buildings, too, though not nearly as many as in the town of Kanesville on the other side of the river. There were people coming across on the ferry all the time, I thought. Then, within a few days, or a few weeks, they left. I wondered if anyone actually lived here.

I kept walking until I found a woman selling used clothing.

"I need a dress or two stout enough to take wagon life," I told her.

She smiled at me, and I saw that she didn't have but three or four of her teeth left. "How about these? A girl brought them in about an hour ago— said she'd outgrown them and she was the youngest." The woman held up a dress made of heavy home-spun cotton and another of flannel. "This one will be best this summer; the flannel is a little bigger for fall," the woman said.

I nodded, pressing the fabric to my face to smell it. It was fresh. Whoever had had the dresses had washed them often enough. The colors were faded a little, but not too bad. "How much?" I asked the woman.

"Fifty cents each." she said.

I laid the dresses back onto her blanket as though they had burned me.

"Now, child," she began, lifting the dresses and handing them back to me. "If that's a little too much—"

"More than a little," I told her.

She shook her head. "Not here it isn't. Everyone here sells high. Including the man who sells me my bread and milk."

She sounded impatient, almost angry. I was sure she heard people gasp and complain all day long about her prices.

I noticed a woman walking past turn her head to look at the dresses. I scooped them back up. "Thirty cents each," I said, imitating my mother's tone of polite stubbornness whenever the tinsmith had come to the door to fix pots.

"All right," the woman said.

I counted out the money and handed it to her, then gathered up the dresses and turned to go— and almost ran into Annie Kyler.

"Katie!" she said, "I thought that was you. Getting ready to leave tomorrow?"

"I'm trying," I answered, not quite sure what I meant.

She rubbed her hands together as though they

were cold. "I am pretty nervous about the whole thing. Three of my sisters stayed home, and I almost wish I had."

"Hiram says we'll be all right," I told her. "And he said your father found a guide."

Annie nodded. "He did. A Mr. Wilkins. The man seems steady to me, considered—not a braggart. I hope so anyway."

I remembered Mr. Barrett and knew what she meant. He had sounded like he knew everything about everything.

Annie smiled. "Do you read?"

I nodded. She put one hand on my shoulder. "Let me show you something."

I followed Annie, staring at all the goods piled on blankets and across the backs of wagons. My mother had loved going into Eldridge on market day. She would have had a picnic here.

I ducked my head. Remembering my mother made my throat ache and my eyes flood with tears. I managed to hide it from Annie by keeping my head turned until I could wipe my eyes.

"Look at these," Annie said, stopping. I turned to see a woman seated on a stool behind four or five wooden crates that were full of periodicals.

"Do you know any of these?" Annie asked.

I read the titles: *The Slave's Friend*—these were old and yellowed and brittle-looking—and *Woodworth's Youth's Cabinet,* and some old *Harper's Magazines*—then I finally saw one I knew. "We read this one in church meeting sometimes," I said, pointing at *The Youth's Companion*. They looked fairly new, too. I bent to read the dates. The top two were only a year old.

"Does it have stories?" Annie asked.

I nodded.

"Perfect," she told me, and gathered up ten or twelve issues. "All you girls will need something to read."

I saw a stack of books to one side of the boxes. *A Christmas Carol*, I read silently. The author's name was Charles Dickens. I bent down and touched the cover. It wasn't leather, and the paper looked tired and worn. My mother had loved singing Christmas carols. I looked up and the woman met my eyes.

"Twenty cents," she said. Her voice was so harsh, so unfriendly, that I didn't even try to bargain with her. I gave her the coins, and I hugged the book against my chest.

Annie smiled as we walked away. "I have a whole box of books in our wagon," she told me. "My father says we'll have to throw them all out to save the oxen before we're done, but I'll carry them myself before I allow that. I cannot imagine a life without my books."

A commotion back in the wagon camps made me turn. I couldn't see anything, but there were shouts and a dog was barking.

"I better get back. I left the Mustang with Hiram," I told Annie.

She touched my arm. "Everything is all right, then. Hiram is that rare kind of man—such a good family man."

I was in such a hurry to get back to the Mustang that I barely heard her. It was only after I was back at the wagon, seeing that the commotion was over a dog fight and that the Mustang was calm, that I thought about what she had said.

Had Hiram talked to the Kylers about his life in New York, about his family? He must have. He had never talked to me about it, except to finally tell me he'd lost them.

I sighed and patted the Mustang's forehead. I

had never talked much about my family. Maybe one of the Kyler girls could become a good enough friend. I felt my eyes stinging. The Kyler girls whispered and laughed and talked to one another all the livelong day. They took turns coddling the white cat and doing chores. What would that be like? I hadn't had a friend my own age since the day I had arrived at Mr. Stevens's house.

The Mustang jerked his head high, and I turned to see two boys racing toward us, chasing a rolling hoop, their push sticks tapping it now and then to keep it going. They veered off in another direction before they got too close, and the Mustang lowered his head to nuzzle my shoulder. I put my arms around his neck and leaned against him for a long minute, listening to their shouts and laughter fade. Then I went back to my chores.

Late in the day, we lined up our wagons for morning. Mr. Wilkins decided on a marching order, and we all went where we were told. Hiram and I ended up near the front of the line. The Kylers brought up the rear, with their big herd of stock behind that.

It took almost two hours, but once we were all

in position, Mr. Wilkins walked up and down the line of wagons, shaking every man's hand and tipping his hat to all the ladies and girls.

Hiram stood off to one side with me, watching. He named the ones he'd met. "Kylers are last, six wagons. The next big party is the Laffertys. Mr. Lafferty has seven wagons; it's a whole family like the Kylers, come here from Philadelphia. Mr. and Mrs. Spengler are between the two groups."

Hiram lifted his hat and slicked his hair back with one hand, then resettled it. "They're from Indiana and have just the one baby. A nephew is driving their second wagon. I had a glimpse inside." He shook his head. "They brought their bedstead, some fancy chairs, a houseful of furniture."

I thought about Mrs. Stevens. Had she gotten to bring any of her grandmother's and mother's things? She would hate the journey, I was sure. There was dirt and grit dust on everything all the time, and no way to keep it back.

When we were finally all lined up, I went and got Midnight and Delia from the Kyler stock. I tethered the mares to the wagon with the Mustang tied loosely beside them. He was content to sleep beside the mares, and I wanted to be able to get a full night's sleep myself.

I lay awake awhile, puzzling on what Annie had said about Hiram. It was hard to imagine him sitting at the Kylers' campfire talking about his family to four or five of them at once. Maybe he had just talked to *Annie* about them. The idea made me uneasy. I wasn't sure why, but it did. I looked at the stars a long time before my eyes finally closed.

CHAPTER EIGHT

❧ ❧ ❧

I have learned to doze, to keep myself from pacing,
but it becomes harder. Too many sounds, too many scents,
all tangled until the air is thick. I often face the wind to
breathe air that smells more of grass and sky.

A storm rolled in during the night, and we all woke to the flash and boom of lightning. The menfolk were up instantly, their suspenders half buttoned, running to try to keep their stock from bolting.

I pulled my dress over my head and sat up, blinking as the sky flickered, long veins of lightning arcing across the darkness. For an instant, the earth was washed in that odd blue light that only comes in a thunderstorm. In that second, I saw everything.

Men were running in every direction. The mares

were standing with their heads up, their eyes rimmed in circles of white, poised to run. The oxen, tethered on a line strung between two scrubby trees, were shifting, uneasy.

The Mustang was rearing. The next flash of blue-white light caught him striking at the sky with his ears flattened against his neck, his teeth bared.

I jumped to the ground behind the wagon, then froze. Without the lightning, the night was ink black, and I could only hear the Mustang snorting, his hooves pounding against the earth.

"Katie!"

It was Hiram's voice.

"I'm here," I shouted back to him. There was no rain yet, but a wind was rising.

"Stay away from the horses!" Hiram shouted at me.

The sky lit a second time, the blue-white flash showing me the Mustang back on all fours. The broken lead rope was dangling from his halter. Then everything went dark for a few seconds.

The next cracking sound overhead was louder than any I had ever heard, and I felt my hair prickling. An eye blink later, there was a crashing roar that shook my whole body. I felt a tremor go through the ground beneath my feet. I clapped my hands over my ears and slumped against the wagon, my heart beating so fast I could barely draw a breath.

The Mustang squealed, and I heard what seemed like dim, distant screams. Hiram was suddenly beside me, his hands on my shoulders, shouting into my face.

"Don't touch that horse. You leave him alone until I get back, do you hear me? If he runs, let him go!"

A lesser bolt of lightning lit up his face for a moment, and I saw a fear in his eyes that scared me worse than I already was.

"It struck somewhere," he was shouting. "Close by—maybe one of the Kylers' wagons!" His grip on my shoulders was painful, and he shook me once, hard. "You stay away from the horse, you hear me? Leave the stock be. I'll be back as soon as I check on Annie."

Then he was gone.

I stood there in the dark, stunned by the storm, by Hiram's shouting at me, but more than anything by his leaving me alone. Trembling, I balled my hands into fists, furious with him for leaving instead of helping me with the Mustang.

The sky flickered with light, and I bit at my lip. The Mustang needed me. Hiram had no right to order me to do *anything*. He was not my father, and I was not bound to obey him by law or by family ties.

The sky flickered again, and I saw the Mustang, trotting in a circle, bucking, then rearing to strike at the sky with his hooves again. His neck was arched, his thick mane streaming in the wind.

The light winked out with a rumble of thunder. Trembling, I made my way around the front of the wagon, my hands guiding me in the darkness. I stepped over the long hickory-wood wagon tongue, then, guiding myself by touching the singletree, tracing the iron rings where the harness straps fastened, then reaching out to find the wheel hub, I straightened up.

I heard the Mustang squeal again. A second or two later, the sky sparkled, then cracked open, pouring the blue-white light over the earth.

"Easy," I said, "Easy, easy..." repeating that single word over and over as I walked toward the

Mustang, pitching my voice so he could hear me over the sound of the dry wind rushing across the ground.

The sky laced with lightning, then darkened, then lit up again. The thunder was less violent each time; the storm was passing us, rolling fast across the land, holding whatever rain it had inside its clouds high above the earth. It didn't even smell like rain... the wind was kicking up dust.

I used every flash of light to get closer to the Mustang. I knew he was watching me, that he was not afraid of me at all. I could also tell that the storm didn't really scare him either. It had only been that crashing, close strike, with the thunder shaking the ground, that had startled him into rearing.

In the next flash of blue-white light, I reached out and caught the broken lead rope in my hand. The Mustang felt the halter pull, and he turned toward me, nuzzling my face and shoulder, then tossing his head and lashing his tail.

I didn't try to lead him anywhere—there was nowhere better to stand that I could think of. The wind was still rising fast, beating the grass flat, whipping my hair and the stallion's mane. It was then that I first smelled smoke. A fire? Who would be fool enough to light a fire in this wind? Then I knew. No one. The lightning had started the blaze.

In between the bolts of lightning, I stared at the sea of wagons around me. There. An orange glow in the dark that should not have been there. I could hear shouts and screams, scattered and dimmed by the dry, rushing wind.

The smell of smoke got stronger, and I could see the tips of orange flame reaching skyward. The fire got brighter, and I saw the silhouettes of people running, gesturing wildly. I knew they were still shouting, but the wind rose a notch, and I couldn't hear anything above it anymore. I wondered if I should try to lead the Mustang and the rest of the stock farther from it.

I hesitated, squinting, trying to figure out how far away the fire was—there was nothing visible to help me judge the distance. For a long time, I stared, afraid that if I looked away, the fire would rush forward. But it didn't. The orange glow diminished and faded and then, finally, it was gone.

The wind slowed a little, and I could hear shouts

again. But they died down fast. Every wagon had a barrel or two of water, every wagon had buckets. People had put the fire out, in spite of the wind. I hoped that no one had been hurt.

I suddenly realized that I was holding a tangled handful of the Mustang's mane in my right hand, and I loosened my fingers to release it. If he had reared again, I might have been dragged under his hooves.

I knew he would never mean to hurt me. He was my friend. Maybe the only real friend I had now. I squinted into the wind, looking for Hiram, but wherever he was, he wasn't worried enough about me to come back and help.

The wind got stronger, coming in gusts, scream-ing through the grass. I pulled on the Mustang's shortened lead rope, gentling him forward a step or two, then another. I walked him toward the mares, dropping the lead rope as he worked his way up beside them and stood close, lowering his muzzle almost to the ground. Both mares had their heads low, using the wagon as a windbreak.

Then I went around to the other side and crawled beneath the wagon bed again. Uneasy, I waited for the sky to light once more so that I could see the end of the broken lead. I crawled forward just far enough to reach it, then ducked back under the shelter of the wagon.

Holding it loosely, I sat beneath the wagon, cross-legged, glad to have Hiram's bedding between me and the dirt, listening to the storm. The worst of it was already past—I could hear thunder in the distance, and, after a few more minutes, the wind brought the faint smell of distant rain.

"Katie!"

It was Hiram's voice. I called back to him, but I knew he hadn't heard me because he shouted again. I didn't answer a second time, because I didn't want to startle the horses. Instead, I released the lead rope and scrambled out from beneath the wagon.

"I'm fine!" I called, and waited for him to get closer so I could ask him if the Kylers were all right and find out what he knew about the fire. But he didn't come closer.

"Good!" he yelled. "I'll be back as quick as I can!" And then he was gone again.

I dragged my pallet out of the wagon bed and wrestled the wind for my blankets. I hauled them beneath the wagon and made a bed of sorts next to Hiram's empty blankets, curling myself up, my back to the wind, the lead rope held loosely in one hand.

The Mustang's lowered muzzle was close enough to touch, and I reached toward him slowly, letting him smell my hand before I dared to brush my fingers across his velvety muzzle. He nibbled at my fingers, licking salt from my skin like an old plow mare.

I closed my eyes and pretended my parents were asleep in the wagon bed above me, my little sister lying between them to keep warm. And somehow, I drifted off to sleep.

CHAPTER NINE

✹ ✹ ✹

The light in the sky struck earth, and something
burned. It scared the little one. I stood close. All the
two-leggeds must understand this. Fire in high wind
terrifies all that live. This fear we all share.

"**K**atie?" It was a woman's voice.

I opened my eyes and felt for the lead rope, then sat up too fast and banged my head on the underside of the wagon bed.

"Be careful."

"I'm all right," I answered, wriggling out from beneath the wagon. The world was still. The wind had gone.

"We thought you might be hungry."

It was Hannah, Andrew's wife. I couldn't remember ever really talking to her; she was usually busy with their baby. "I came to offer you breakfast," she said.

"Is Hiram all right?" I asked, suddenly worried.

Hannah nodded. "I think he dozed off. He stayed up most the night with Annie."

"Is she hurt?" I asked, finally understanding why Hiram hadn't come back—but if Annie had sprained an ankle jumping from a wagon gate or something, she had more than a dozen people to take care of her. I didn't have another except Hiram.

I saw a worried look come into Hannah's eyes. "Her hands are burned badly. She ran to help with the fire. I'm not sure yet how it happened, but I know four wagons just upwind from ours burned to ashes."

I swallowed hard, feeling guilty. "Whose wagons?"

"Three belonged to the family from Philadelphia. I don't know the other people—they weren't part of our party, but the sparks flew in a wind gust and…"

Hannah trailed off, her voice heavy with weariness and worry. I glanced at the Mustang. He was half dozing, his weight on three legs. The mares were calm and still. Their tether lines were tied to the wagon. The oxen were asleep.

"Will you come?" Hannah asked me again.

The whole camp was pretty quiet. Not many people were awake yet. It made sense. Most of them had probably barely slept the whole night long; they would rise a little later than usual.

"I can't be gone too long," I told Hannah.

She nodded. "Just long enough to eat. My mother promised Hiram she'd look after you."

I walked beside Hannah as we started off, trying to smooth my dirty dress a little, but the cloth was creased from sleeping in it.

"We all look pretty dirty today," Hannah said. "No one will notice."

I glanced at her. She was smiling at me. I tried to smile back, but I couldn't. One storm had changed everything.

"Annie is in her parents' wagon," Hannah said. She pointed, then smiled a little. "Mary is the one cooking this morning—she sent me after you."

A few seconds after she said it, I could smell the bacon, and my mouth watered. My stomach suddenly caved in, and I realized how hungry I was.

I let Hannah lead the way as we threaded a path through the wagons and the stock, making our way back down the line. I nodded politely to anyone I saw up and about, trying to remember the names Hiram had told me, but the wind had blown them away along with everything else.

I caught a glimpse of the burned wagons on the flat, trampled ground. People circled the ashes aimlessly, as though they still could not believe what had happened. My heart ached for them. Everything they owned was gone, and I had no idea what they would do. I only hoped no one else had been hurt.

Mrs. Kyler was bent over a cook fire. She straightened up to press one hand against the small of her back and saw me coming. "Hello, Katie."

"Where's Hiram?" I asked. Then I realized how rude I was being. "Thank you for inviting me to breakfast, ma'am," I said politely. I raked one hand back through my hair and had to pull my fingers free from the tangles.

"We can all use a hairbrush this morning," she said when she saw me blushing. "I'll loan you mine after you eat."

I nodded and thanked her again.

"Hiram fell asleep watching over Annie. She's in our wagon—two back down the line." She sighed heavily and wiped at her eyes. I could tell she was trying not to weep. "I thought I'd cook up here," she added, "spare Annie some of the noise and commotion... maybe she can rest better."

I had no idea what to say. I hadn't wanted to ask her how bad Annie's burns were, and now I wouldn't have to. I could tell from Mrs. Kyler's voice that she was really worried.

I heard girls' voices and saw curly dark hair through the keyhole-shaped opening in a wagon cover. It was one of the little girls—Hope? Maybe. I saw Julia's long dark braids for an instant, then they all moved away from the opening.

I exhaled, my own weariness settling on my shoulders. I still couldn't keep most of the Kyler cousins straight. I heard a round of shushing and whispering inside the wagon, and I wished I *did* know all their names, that I knew them better. But they played with one another, not with me.

I wondered what kind of games they played, and an odd feeling came over me. I didn't really know how to play anymore. Losing my family to the fever and living with Mr. and Mrs. Stevens had scraped my spirits so thin that I had forgotten how.

Mrs. Kyler was looking at me. "Andrew tells me

you're going to let my boys run the Mustang as part of our herd so you can have a little more time to yourself."

I turned and looked at her, suddenly angry. "Some days, maybe. I don't know yet," I said, keeping my voice as polite as I could. "The Mustang trusts me. I have to be careful with him."

She nodded and pushed her hair from her face. "Well, you can trust Andrew and the boys. They are all fine horse hands."

I watched as she turned back to stir the bacon in the deep pan of popping lard. "Hungry?"

"Yes, ma'am," I answered, grateful to be fed but resenting it, too. I wanted Hiram to come back to our wagon. We could cook. We could eat without imposing on the Kylers.

Another round of whispering came from inside the wagon, and one by one the girls tumbled out, tiptoeing around the side of the big wagon, off on some adventure that they didn't want their grandmother to notice.

"There you are!"

I looked up. Hiram was walking toward me. His clothes were even rougher than mine. His hickory shirt was covered in black soot and dirt, and his face was smudged.

"Someone tell you Annie got hurt?" he asked me.

I nodded. "Hannah came and got me. I'm real sorry to hear it, Hiram. Will she mend all right?"

He walked me a little ways from the cook fire. "She was trying to help put out the blaze," Hiram said, wonderingly. "Imagine. She's about as big as a minute, and she just leapt into that bucket line. Oh, Katie, her poor hands..." He stopped and looked at me closely. "You're all right? The Mustang?"

"I held on to him. I know you told me not to, but it was fine. He's standing quiet with the mares—he was steady all night, even in the wind."

Hiram rubbed his face with both hands and heaved in a long breath. "Well," he finally said. "The Kylers won't be going anywhere today or tomorrow, and I think we should wait with them."

I nodded. I hadn't thought about it, but it only made sense. "Will everyone wait?"

Hiram shrugged. "I doubt it. Mr. Wilkins can find more people to go."

I didn't answer. I was sure he was right.

Hiram kicked at the dirt. "There are hundreds

of people looking for guides. And everyone knows that a day or two delay can mean trouble at the end." He sighed. "Wilkins was the only one we all liked. It took a lot of talk and some arguments before we settled on him."

I nodded.

"You angry at me?" Hiram sounded so tired and so discouraged that I didn't answer. What could I say? I wasn't angry, really—I was something else. Something I couldn't put a name on. He shifted his weight, shrugging his shoulders up high to stretch.

"Katie?" Mrs. Kyler called. "Food's ready!"

"You better go get something to eat," he said gently, reaching out to brush the top of my head the way he always had when he could tell I was upset.

"When are you coming back to the wagon?" I asked him.

He looked at me and started to say something, then didn't speak for another half minute. When he did, he sounded so sad and weary it scared me. "I'll be back by afternoon, I think. I want to wait for Annie to wake up."

I nodded again. What else could I do?

"Food's ready, Katie!" Mrs. Kyler called.

"Give Annie my best wishes," I said.

Hiram thanked me, then his face collapsed into pain and worry. "Katie, it's bad. She can barely stand the pain, and her right hand might be curled up, crippled."

His voice was hollow as a blade of straw. I felt a chill, remembering the shouting, the screams. Had it been Annie? "Oh, Hiram, I hope it isn't that bad," I said aloud.

"Katie?" Mrs. Kyler called again.

"I'm sorry," I told Hiram. "I'm so sorry it happened."

He nodded and then turned away. I walked toward the campfire, feeling light-headed and strange. I pressed my lips together.

Mrs. Kyler was bustling around, pretending to be cheerful. I had a lot of practice at that kind of pretending, and I was grateful to her. I admired her. It was her daughter lying in the wagon with burned hands.

I tried not to eat like a wolf this time, even though I saw Ralph and Andrew waiting for plates. The eggs and bacon tasted like heaven, though, and it was hard to eat politely. Sitting there, chewing, my stomach filling up, I began to feel a little better. The moment I was finished eating, Mrs. Kyler took my plate and rinsed it for one of her sons to use. I thanked her twice and she smiled at me, but I could see the strain in her eyes. She was terribly worried about Annie.

When I got back to our wagon, I shook the dust and grass out of the bedding and spread it to air. Then I walked the Mustang and the mares out of camp until I found a good patch of new grass. Only once they were grazing—and I was well away from anyone who might overhear—did I tell the Mustang about everything that had happened. He listened, nudging me gently a few times as if he understood and was sorry.

After a few hours, I took the horses back. The oxen were shifting, walking the tether line back and forth. They had eaten every blade of grass they could reach. I had helped my father herd oxen when I was six years old. I had watched Hiram with these animals, and they both seemed placid enough. If I didn't graze them, they'd pull the line down and go on their own before long.

I looked around. If Hiram had been to the wagon, I saw no sign of it. Before I left again, I wrote a note to leave on the wagon seat, weighting it down with a stone.

I got my new book out of my blanket bundle and set it out, then freed the oxen from the tether line. I tucked the book beneath my arm, then walked around behind them, clapping my hands. They began to move away from me slowly, staying together. Once they were moving, I ran back and got the horses again, leading the mares and letting the Mustang follow.

I held the horses back and let the oxen set their own pace. I saw a number of people turn to watch them go by, their white-splotched coats smooth and shiny in the sun. Hiram had made a real find, it looked like. Between the oxen and the Mustang, we got a lot of stares.

I lost my nervousness as we went. The oxen responded slowly and calmly to anything I did. The horses were full of grass and enjoying the sun. None of them knew the country any better than I did, so they were content to let me decide our direction. I finally found good grass almost a mile from the camp and settled under a tree to read while they all grazed.

A Christmas Carol wasn't at all what I had expected. It was exciting, almost scary. Mr. Dickens had written a story about a mean man and ghosts that came every night in his dreams...and I was still so tired that I dozed off twice and had to rouse myself and walk around. I couldn't sleep. I had to watch the stock.

An hour before dusk, I walked the oxen back to the wagon camp. Hiram was not there. My note was where I had left it.

I refolded all the aired bedding and unrolled my blanket bundle once more. I replaced the new book, then stood staring at my mother's old fairy storybook. I held it for a long time. I even unwrapped the cloth and took out the silver shoe buckles that had belonged to my father. I kept expecting to cry, but I didn't. I think I was just too tired.

I bedded down beneath the wagon again, even though the storm was long gone. The Mustang lowered his head and reached around the wheel to nudge me once or twice before he settled into sleep.

CHAPTER TEN

✿ ✿ ✿

*I am tired of this crowded place. Even the grass
tastes of the two-leggeds' food, their bodies, their scents.
It is time to travel on.*

*T*he next day, Mr. Wilkins left with a full
party of wagons. All the Kylers and Hiram and
I stayed back. Annie was in so much pain that moving the wagon she was in—even just to get out of
line—made her scream once or twice. But she was
too weak to walk and had to lie down. I saw her for
a moment. Her face was white as next-day ashes.
It scared me to look at her. Hiram looked like the
pain was his own. I watched as the Kylers made their
new camp. He rarely left her side.

The Kylers made a half circle of the wagons a half

mile to the north of the ferry. Hiram helped me move our stock and wagon close by, then he left again. He ate and slept in the Kylers' camp for the next few days, keeping Annie company. He came to our wagon once or twice a day to check on me.

He was proud of me for taking over and grazing the stock. He said I was as good a helper as any girl had ever been. But he didn't eat with me, and I slept alone in our little camp. He went back to sit with Annie.

I ate supper at the Kylers' fire for those first few days, too. I cooked my own bacon in the mornings, and it was handier—I could get the animals out to graze earlier if I cooked for myself. But it was lonely and cold, too.

"Annie is a little better," Hiram said on the third evening. "There are places where her skin was burned black, and it is falling away." He drew in a breath, his eyes still full of worry. Then he nodded and went on, talking fast, as if he were reassuring himself. "The wound isn't putrifying. There's no fever. With rest, I think she will heal. We found a man who knows some doctoring, and he said as much."

I lowered my eyes. "I hope so, Hiram."

"Katie?"

His voice had changed, and I looked at him. "Yes?"

"Are you set on going west?"

My heart skipped a beat. "Yes," I said quietly. "Oh, yes. I have to find my uncle and his family, Hiram. You know that."

Hiram nodded. The he blew out a breath in one whoosh, like a man who has picked up something he is barely able to lift. "I'd best get back to Annie," he said. Then he walked away.

I watched him go. It was pretty clear he had taken a real fancy to Annie. Probably, once she was healing, he would want to take her in our little wagon, not me. Maybe that was why he asked about my going west. Maybe he wanted to leave me somewhere, like Mr. Stevens had planned to do.

I barely tasted my supper, and I noticed Mrs. Kyler watching me, but she didn't say anything when I left even earlier than usual.

Back at our little wagon that night, I tried to read, but I ended up listening to the Kylers singing around their campfire. I could hear them talking;

I could hear Polly and Julia and the other girls playing and laughing. I pressed my lips together so tightly my mouth began to ache.

I didn't want to cry. I knew it wouldn't help me one little bit. But the tears began to roll down my face, and I couldn't do anything about them. I went to stand beside the Mustang in the darkness, leaning against his shoulder until the crying faded into sniffles and shuddery sighs.

"I want my family back," I whispered to the Mustang. "I just want to *belong* somewhere."

He shook his mane and stamped one back hoof. I dragged in a long breath and let it out slowly. Then I stepped back and set about laying out my bedding for the night.

The next morning dawned clear and bright. I ate a biscuit from the tin and a little salt bacon, raw. I didn't have time to make a fire. I gathered up the horses and drove them and the oxen out to find grass. It was getting harder to find places that hadn't been grazed flat. I finally found a good little meadow, but it took me a few hours, so I had to stay late to let the animals eat their fill.

When I got back to the wagon, it was almost dark.

There was a note on the wagon seat. It said: *Join us for supper, Katie, please.*

No one had signed it, but I was pretty sure Hiram had left it. Or maybe Mrs. Kyler had sent one of the girls to leave it for me. In any case, I was grateful. I was tired, and I hadn't eaten much for breakfast and nothing for dinner. I didn't want to rekindle a fire and cook, and I had begun to feel uncomfortable just showing up for a meal without being invited.

I tethered the mares and tied the Mustang loosely to one of the wagon wheels. The oxen took longer. They were sleepy and slow and didn't want to be led anywhere. By the time I got their leads tied to the tether line, the stars were out.

"We found a good guide," I heard Mr. Kyler saying as I walked through the darkness toward the big Kyler camp. "His name is Teal. He's looking for more wagons, but he wants to leave tomorrow. He says we are already risking snow at the other end."

"They all say that," Andrew said quietly. His brothers Charles and Ralph were nodding as I stepped into the circle of light from their cook fire and wagon lanterns. Not one person noticed me. This was a serious talk. I stood close to one of the wagons and listened.

Mr. Kyler shrugged. "So do the guidebooks. It's true. We're almost ten days behind what we meant to be."

"If you like him, Pa," Andrew said, "I think we should go. Waiting is foolish if Annie can travel now."

At that, everyone turned, and I followed their eyes. Annie was sitting next to Hiram on a blanket near a second campfire. She smiled, but she didn't speak.

Mr. Kyler looked at his sons. "Andrew? Charles? Ralph? You think we should go?"

They all nodded. Mr. Kyler looked across the fire at his daughter and her husband. "Henry, you think we should?" His son-in-law nodded and murmured in agreement. Then he looked at Hiram.

"I can be ready," Hiram said. "Katie has kept the stock in grand shape, and she's got the wagon packed."

Mr. Kyler looked at his wife last. "Mary?"

She made a shooing motion with her hand. "I'm ready. Or nearly. We aren't the ones to ask. It's up to Annie."

All the eyes went back to Annie, and she smiled

again and nodded this time. Hiram rested one hand on her shoulder for an instant, and she looked up at him. Her skin was the color of the moon, still. I saw her leaning on Hiram's arm.

"Tomorrow, then," Mr. Kyler said. "I'll go tell Mr. Teal he has seven more wagons."

Andrew whooped, and a ragged cheer rose from the men. The whole Kyler family was celebrating the decision. I kept quiet, but I was as excited as anyone else. The sooner I got to Oregon, the sooner I could celebrate with my own family.

CHAPTER ELEVEN

❦ ❦ ❦

The little one makes sounds I cannot understand.
I know she needs me to stand close, and so I do. Sometimes
that is the only thing that can be done—to make sure
that no one stands alone in the wind or the dark.

I packed, repacked, checked everything in the wagon, and made sure the harness and ox yokes were stacked without tangles. I went to bed beneath our little wagon that night feeling better than I had since the night of the fire. Everything was going to be all right after all. Annie was doing better. She would have a hard time at first on the trail, I was sure. But her mother and her family would all take care of her. Hiram would tend her in the evenings. I would help any way I could.

I sighed and rolled over in my blankets. I was

excited and scared and relieved—so many feelings were jostling inside me that I lay awake for a long time. Finally, the throbbing of the crickets put me to sleep.

"Katie?"

"What?" I rolled over when Hiram said my name. I peered out from under the wagon, blinking, surprised to see him outlined against a grayish sky. The night had passed. The sun would be up in an hour.

"We're all ready," I told him, yawning.

He was shaking his head. "Katie, get up and get dressed. I need you to come with me for a few minutes."

He turned his back while I pulled my dress on over my camisole and found my shoes. I crawled out from under the wagon and glanced at the Mustang. He was awake, watching me, but his head was lowered, and the mares were still asleep.

"He'll be fine, Katie," Hiram said.

Shivering a little in the morning chill, I followed Hiram as he walked toward the Kylers' camp. He walked fast.

"What's wrong?" I asked, running to catch up. Hiram didn't answer. He just pointed.

I looked past him. The campfire was barely burning. No one else was up and about yet, but Annie was sitting in a chair set beside her parents' wagon. Her hands were wrapped in balls of white cloth. She was slumped over until she saw us. Then she sat up straight and smiled at me—a soft, apologetic smile.

Hiram took my hand and led me forward. I could feel my heart beating inside my chest. Annie's face was tight with pain.

"Katie," she began as soon as I was close, "I hope you will forgive me." Her voice was almost a whisper—she was trying not to wake anyone else this early.

She hesitated then. My mind raced ahead of her words. Maybe she and Hiram had decided to marry as soon as she was better, and she was about to explain that they had decided they didn't want to raise an orphan girl. Maybe Hiram had found some local boardinghouse woman who needed a girl to help out.

I was scared—and I was angry. It was so mean to tell me at the last possible minute. "I won't stay here," I whispered back, without meaning to speak at all. "You can't make me stay. I have worked hard and I—"

Hiram gestured at me to be quiet, and Annie's eyes widened.

"Even if you think someone is nice and wants to take me in, I won't stay here," I went on. "I'm going west with you no matter what."

Hiram cleared his throat. "Katie."

I glanced up at him, and he shook his head slightly, his face full of unhappiness.

"It's not you who has to stay, Katie," Annie said quietly. "It's me." She held up her bandaged hands. "It hurts so much, Katie. I can't sleep, I can't eat or work; I can't help with *anything*. I can't even wash myself or feed myself or..." She began to cry. Hiram stood closer to her then, stroking her hair as she wept.

"Her family will all stay behind with her," Hiram said. He looked up at the gray sky, then back at me. "Unless I do."

I let out a long breath, understanding why he had gotten me up, why the decision was last minute. They had probably been talking half the night with her brothers and her parents.

"And you want to stay with her," I said, just so he wouldn't have to say it.

He smiled. "I do. I have asked Annie if she will marry me."

Annie lifted her head and looked at me through her tears. "Katie, I am so sorry to make things harder for you. I know you want to go, but if you decide to stay with us, you are most welcome. Hiram thinks the world of you."

"Thank you kindly," I said, trying to gather my scattered thoughts.

"If you want to go," Annie added, "my folks will see you safely to Oregon." Her eyes were round with tears and pain, and she lifted her arm to wipe her face on her sleeve and winced in agony. It was such an awkward gesture, so clumsy because of her bandaged hands, that I was ashamed for being angry. She wanted to go west with her family. She couldn't.

Hiram was looking at me. "Annie didn't decide until about a half hour ago. It has been very hard for her. We woke you early to give you some time to think at least. To decide for yourself."

I felt almost light-headed. The night was still and dark, and none of this felt quite real to me. "I need a little time alone," I told them both. I dragged in a long breath and felt myself trembling.

"Thank you both," I managed. "Annie, you know I wish you and Hiram well." I looked at him. "Hiram, I am so happy you are…" I trailed off because I had no idea how to say what I meant.

He smiled and finished for me. "In love. I am in love again."

I nodded. Then I turned and made my way back to the wagon. I saw a few people peek out of the Kylers' wagons as I passed. I ran the last little way and saw the Mustang watching me, his head up and his eyes alert.

I slowed enough not to startle him, then walked closer to put my arms around his neck, pressing my face against his coat. He shook his mane, and it cascaded down, covering my face and my shoulder. I closed my eyes. I wanted to keep them closed, to never move, to hide forever.

For the longest time, I stood there, just leaning on the Mustang, wishing I could disappear and never have to decide anything ever again.

When I finally stepped back, I began to talk to the Mustang, explaining everything that had happened. "I want to go," I finished. "But the Kylers all have their own families, and none of the girls like me.

And I'll have to sleep in or near their wagons and see them all the time and—"

The sound of someone softly clearing his throat made me whirl around. It was Hiram.

The sky was getting lighter. I could see the strain on his face. He was exhausted, and he wanted desperately to have things turn out as well as they could. He cared about me. He loved Annie, but he cared about me, too.

"Annie asked me to tell you that everyone just wants you to do what you feel is right," he said.

"I want to go." The words just came out of my mouth, and I knew they were true. I had to find my real family. I *needed* to find them.

Hiram nodded. "Then you should. You can take most of the supplies. The Kylers will fit in the bacon and the rest." He looked into my face. "Are you sure?"

The Mustang tossed his head, then rubbed his cheek on my shoulder. I tangled my fingers in his mane. I felt so lost. It wasn't like I was leaving my home again. I had no home, not in any real way. But I was leaving Hiram. Annie was right. He was a good man. But the only family I had was in Oregon, and

I had to find them or my whole life would be like this... leaving places that weren't really home. The idea of never belonging anywhere terrified me.

"I'm going," I said quietly. Then I cleared my throat and said it more clearly.

Hiram didn't answer for a moment. When he did, his voice was kind. "I'll tell them all. You need to get your things moved. Teal is starting to line up the wagons."

"I'll make it quick," I promised.

And I did. Hiram helped me. It took less than ten minutes to get my share of the foodstuffs to the Kylers' wagon. My blanket bundle fit beneath a pile of Mrs. Kyler's quilts. I washed my face and hands from our barrel of water, then led the mares over to Andrew. He was holding the stock, letting them mill in circles, grazing on the beaten grass of the clearing.

Hiram hitched up the oxen and moved the wagon over toward the line, but not too close. He found a spot beneath a cottonwood tree.

Two of Annie's brothers formed a chair by join-ing arms. Annie sat in it, an arm around each of their shoulders as they carried her across the grass to the little wagon. Andrew came behind, bringing her chair. Once she was seated comfortably where she could watch her family depart, Hiram and her brothers moved her things from the Kylers' wagon into Hiram's.

The camp buzzed like a kicked beehive as the Kylers prepared to leave. Mrs. Kyler ran to give Annie another quilt and began another long, tearful good-bye. Hannah, Ellen, and the rest took turns hugging her. Her brothers kept finding reasons to ask her something, to stand beside her and touch her hair. They were all afraid of the same thing, I knew. Few people undertook the risk of this journey twice. They might never see Annie again.

I stood near the Kylers' wagon, waiting, trying to stay out of the way. Then Hiram found me, and I walked the Mustang over to our little wagon for the last time. "I will be proud if Annie and I ever have a daughter as strong and brave as you are, Katie," he said.

I tried not to cry. I hugged Hiram, and Annie tipped her head so I could kiss her on her cheek. "I promise to repay you one day for the provisions and everything else," I told Hiram.

He took my hands in his and looked into my face. "Katie, you have given me back everything that ever mattered to me. You thawed my heart." I stood very still and watched him step back to place his hand on Annie's shoulder.

"And I will always be grateful for that," Annie whispered.

At that instant, the sun broke over the horizon, spreading yellow-gold light across the grass.

The Mustang nuzzled at my shoulder, and I squared my shoulders. "I have to go," I told Hiram and Annie.

We all held back tears as they wished me well, then I led the Mustang back toward the wagons. He whinnied once, a shrill, piercing call. The mares answered him from where they stood in Andrew Kyler's herd of stock.

I followed the Kylers' wagons heading toward the line that was forming. The Mustang pranced along beside me, never pulling on the lead rope, but dancing sideways, then back, his neck arched. The ox teams plodded forward slowly, deliberately, as though they were alone in understanding what two thousand miles really meant.